THE AUDITION

Also by **Maddie Ziegler**

The Maddie Diaries

MADDIE ZIEGLER

THE AUDITION

with Julia DeVillers

ALADDIN
New York London Toronto Sydney New Delhi

This book is a work of fiction. Any references to historical events, real people, or real places are used fictitiously. Other names, characters, places, and events are products of the author's imagination, and any resemblance to actual events or places or persons, living or dead, is entirely coincidental.

ALADDIN

An imprint of Simon & Schuster Children's Publishing Division

1230 Avenue of the Americas, New York, New York 10020

First Aladdin hardcover edition October 2017

Text copyright © 2017 by M, M and M, Inc.

Jacket illustrations copyright © 2017 by Magdalina Dianova

All rights reserved, including the right of reproduction in whole or in part in any form.

ALADDIN and related logo are registered trademarks of Simon & Schuster, Inc.

For information about special discounts for bulk purchases, please contact Simon & Schuster Special Sales at 1-866-506-1949 or business@simonandschuster.com.

The Simon & Schuster Speakers Bureau can bring authors to your live event. For more information or to book an event contact the Simon & Schuster Speakers Bureau at 1-866-248-3049 or visit our website at www.simonspeakers.com.

Book designed by Laura Lyn DiSiena

The text of this book was set in Miller Text.

Manufactured in the United States of America 0917 FFG

10 9 8 7 6 5 4 3 2 1

Library of Congress Cataloging-in-Publication Data

Names: Ziegler, Maddie, author. | DeVillers, Julia, author.

Title: The audition / by Maddie Ziegler with Julia DeVillers.

Description: First Aladdin hardcover edition. | New York : Aladdin, 2017. |

Series: Maddie Ziegler ; 1 | Summary: Twelve-year-old Harper loves to dance and is a rising star in Connecticut when her parents move her to Florida and she must prove herself to The Bunheads in order to compete.

Identifiers: LCCN 2017017478 (print) | LCCN 2017035695 (eBook) |

ISBN 9781481486385 (eBook) | ISBN 9781481486361 (hc) |

Subjects: | CYAC: Dance—Fiction. | Competition (Psychology)—Fiction. | Cliques (Sociology)—Fiction. | Moving, Household—Fiction. | Family life—Florida—Fiction. | Florida—Fiction. | BISAC: JUVENILE FICTION / Performing Arts / Dance. | JUVENILE FICTION / Social Issues / Friendship. | JUVENILE FICTION / Social Issues / New Experience.

Classification: LCC PZ7.1.Z54 (eBook) | LCC PZ7.1.Z54 Aud 2017 (print) | DDC [Fic]—dc23

LC record available at https://lccn.loc.gov/2017017478

THE AUDITION

I'm standing just offstage, waiting for my big moment. I know my mom and dance teacher are in the audience, holding their breath in anticipation. This will be the most challenging dance I've ever performed—not only that but the most challenging dance anyone at DanceStarz Academy has ever performed. There's a lot of pressure on me.

My costume is amazing—beautifully detailed with thousands of sparkling rhinestones—my makeup is flawless, and my headpiece is sewn in tightly but not so tightly it will give me a screaming headache later.

"You can do it, Harper! Love you, Harper!" My new teammates are encouraging, but I know they're questioning how

this will go. This routine is nearly impossible! How could any twelve-year-old ever possibly pull this off? My adrenaline is racing.

The announcer says:

"Please welcome to the stage: Harper McCoy, performing a solo."

I walk onto the stage, my toes pointed, my head held high. I get into my opening pose and the music begins. Five . . . six . . . seven . . . eight!

And I dance! I'm in the zone as I leap and turn and flip and practically fly. The crowd is gasping. I'm nailing it! And I go into my grand finale: my new signature turn series. I do an insane number of tuck jumps and pirouettes. Twirling, twirling, twirling . . .

The crowd is going wild! The audience is chanting: "Harper! Harper!" My mother's voice in particular stands out from the crowd.

"Harper! Harper!" Mom was whispering loudly. "Stop twirling!"

What? Stop *twirling?*

I opened my eyes and snapped out of my daydream.

"You're twirling your hair," Mom said quietly.

Oops. I was spacing out. I let go of the piece of hair I was twisting from my ponytail. I wasn't onstage at a competition, amazing the audience. I wasn't even on a competition team— yet. I was sitting in a new chair, in a new dance studio, waiting to audition for a totally new competition team.

"Oh, no!" My eight-year-old sister, Hailey, dramatically fake-gasped and pointed at me from the couch across from me. "It's the apocalypse! Harper has . . . *wispies*!"

My hand flew to the top of my head to smooth any wispies that might have escaped my tight ponytail. I wanted this audition to go perfectly, and that included the details that could distract the judges, like flyaway hair.

"I'm just kidding!" Hailey laughed. "Please. Like Harper didn't use half a can of hairspray this morning."

"Hailey, now isn't a good time for teasing. Your sister is nervous."

"Harper, are you nervous?" Hailey asked.

Um . . . YES?!!

I was about to audition for a new dance studio. I'd be placed in classes (what if I choked and they stuck me in beginner classes with teeny five-year-olds in tutus?) and I'd find out if I could be on a competition team. So, basically my entire life.

Okay, maybe that sounded overly dramatic. But dancing was my life. The dance studio had been my second home since

I was two years old. My mom always said that when I was really little, I would dress up like a fairy princess or a butterfly and jump and twirl around and break things, so she signed me up for a little-kid ballet class to get rid of all that energy. I'd been at that studio ever since.

I took every class they offered: ballet, jazz, tap, lyrical, contemporary. I loved lyrical and contemporary the most, felt confident with my technique in ballet classes, and did tumbling and hip-hop for fun and to help with my routines.

I joined the precompetitive team when I was six and then made the junior competition team. Last year, I started getting solos—and winning with them. My BFFs were on the team with me, and we practiced together almost every day after school.

Don't get me wrong—I liked doing other things besides dancing: drawing, painting, baking brownies, hanging out with my friends, and watching funny YouTube videos (and videos of dancers like Travis Wall and Maddie Ziegler). But the dance floor was my happy place.

A few weeks ago, Dad got a new job in Florida and we had to move pretty quickly.

I cried for a week when Mom and Dad told me; Hailey cried for a week too; even my Mom cried when we packed up our stuff. I definitely didn't want to leave. Eventually, Hailey and Mom said they were up for the adventure of it, but me? I didn't want to say good-bye to my friends and my old life. I didn't want to say good-bye to my old dance studio.

Or hello to a new studio. And new friends.

At least, I *hoped* I'd have a new dance studio. There was a chance they wouldn't even take me on a competition team. When I told my dance teacher back in Connecticut I was moving, she told me that dance was a huge part of Florida culture. That sounded great! Then she told me that Florida had a highly competitive dance community. *HIGHLY* competitive. Eep.

So yeah. I was nervous about this audition at DanceStarz.

"Harper, don't put too much pressure on yourself," Mom said. "If this studio isn't a fit, we can try another one. I just thought since DanceStarz is a newer studio that has only been open a few years, it might be easier for you to acclimate. Be a big fish in a smaller pond."

"Harperfish." Hailey sucked in her cheeks to make a fish face at me. She cracked herself up.

"Also," Mom continued, "DanceStarz is the most convenient to our new house. There's only a few weeks left of summer break, and once school starts, I want to find a job and it would be hard to drive you far. Plus, the other studios have already had competition team tryouts. We're lucky Dance-Starz is letting newcomers audition. Well, worst-case scenario, you could wait until next year. . . ."

"Not helpful, Mom." I raised an eyebrow at her.

"Oh, I'm babbling, aren't I?" My mom smiled at me. "I'm sorry. I just want what's best for you."

I knew my mom got nervous for me too. I did appreciate my mom. Not only did she drive me to the studio practically every day, she had to do things like hot-glue thousands of rhinestones on competition costumes at the last minute and sew my hair into bizarre headpieces with feathers or things while I yelped in pain.

"Mom!" Hailey waved to get my mom's attention. "I need to get something from the car."

"Now?" Mom sighed, then turned to me. "Are you okay alone for a minute?"

"Yes!" Remember how I said I appreciate my dance mom? I also appreciate having her leave—so I can get into my head and into the dance zone, I mean.

I looked around the reception area as I waited. There was a huge DanceStarz logo above the main desk. DanceStarz colors were pink, white, and gold, which I had to admit looked pretty cool. DanceStarz was much brighter than my old studio, with white walls and huge floor-to-ceiling windows. (It was particularly strange to look out the window and see palm trees.)

"Harper!" The woman working the front desk called my name. "Vanessa will see you in fifteen minutes. You may get ready and stretch in Studio C. It's the first door on the left down the corridor."

Here we go.

ive, six, seven, eight.

I counted off as if I were about to start a dance routine while I walked toward the room where my fate would be determined. I passed a vending machine and water fountain as I made my way down the hallway. It was bright too, with the Florida sun streaming in through the windows. I passed Studio A, a huge studio lined with more windows, and Studio B, a smaller one. Nobody was in either of them.

And I reached Studio C.

As I walked in, the scent of the dance studio hit me—a scent that any dancer in the world would recognize: sweaty feet. It smelled like home. Stinky, but like home.

This was smaller than the other two rooms I'd seen. Nobody was in here, either. I slipped out of my white tank and shorts so that I was wearing a black leotard, my most comfortable one, with the crisscross straps in the back.

I could see my reflection in the three mirrored walls of the studio. Oh. Hailey was right. I did have the dreaded wispies. I decided to put my hair up in a dance bun. No wispies, and it would give me something to do to take my mind off my audition. I was an expert at dance buns. I'd done them so many times, I could do it with my eyes closed.

I unzipped my dance duffel. Inside, I had packed all the dance necessities:

Bobby pins

Hairspray

Hair elastics

Extra leotard (black with cami straps)

Tights—pink, in case I had to do ballet

Hairbrush

Bandages

Tape for my feet

Toe pads for my pointe shoes

Water bottle

Packet of trail mix

Towel, because you get sweaty when you dance hard

Deodorant, because see above

Stretch band

And, of course, I'd had to pack a lot of shoes: my ballet shoes, pointe shoes, jazz and tap shoes. Even though I was going to do a contemporary routine for my audition, I wanted to be extra prepared.

I had also brought a few other things:

Vanilla-scented spray (Remember the stinky studio? A quick spritz of this and at least *I* smelled better).

Fuzzy socks with grippers to keep my feet warm. Black-and-white-striped with a zebra face on the toes. I know, super cute!

Pins stuck on the outside of the bag that my dance team friends had given me as going-away presents to remember them forever and always! Except—sorry, guys—right now I had to forget about them. I had to focus on my future. Not just focus—*hyper*focus, and dance my heart out.

I grabbed some hairpins and my hairspray from the bag and went to the mirror to put my long, medium-brown hair up into a bun. I redid my ponytail (no wispies!) and twisted it into a tight "rope." I wrapped the "rope" around the hair elastic, flattening it out a little and securing it with hairpins—lots of hairpins. Then I tucked the end under tightly and pinned it some more. I finished with a heavy dose of hairspray to freeze it into place.

Bun was done.

I unzipped the shoe compartment, stuck in my flip-flops, and pulled out my half-soles. These were shoes that covered the top half of my feet and had a strap across them but were open at the heel. These were the best shoes for a variety of dance styles, like contemporary or lyrical, so I wouldn't slip on the floor. I sat down on the rubbery marley floor and pulled on a shoe. I winced as I hit a blister, but pulled the shoe on all the way. Blisters came with the territory. So did sore muscles, scabs, and bruises. Us dancers are tough.

I was ready to stretch. As any teacher will tell you a million times, because it's true, stretching warms up muscles, increases flexibility, and helps prevent injuries. I stood up and began with neck rolls. I could see myself in the mirror as I rolled my head to the left and then to the right. Then I did some shoulder rolls.

Just as I started side stretches, the door opened.

And a giant trophy walked in—with my little sister's legs and slightly lighter-than-mine brown pigtails sticking out from behind it. *Oh my gosh. Hailey.* That trophy was almost as big as she was.

"Weeeeeee are the champions, my friend!" the trophy sang. "And we'll keep on fighting—"

"Hailey, what are you doing with my trophy?" I asked her. "And what are you doing in here?!"

"You were nervous, so I'm reminding you who you are. You're a champion dancer!" Hailey triumphantly placed the trophy on the floor in front of me. "Like it says on the plaque. *Top Junior Solo of the World.*"

"Not exactly the world." I had to grin. "At nationals."

"Oh. Actually, I never really read the plaque. Well, nationals is still pretty good, I guess," Hailey reassured me.

Nationals was more than pretty good. It was amazing! It was held in New Jersey, so close to New York City you could see skyscrapers through the windows of the convention center. I had danced a lyrical solo. I'd loved my intricate choreography, the beautiful music, and my shimmery costume. After I'd danced, I'd watched the crowd jump up from their seats and cheer. Including my mom and sister. My sister might be annoying, but she really was my biggest cheerleader.

"Thanks, Hailey. Seriously," I said. "But now, please hide the trophy, and you need to go!"

"Hide it?" Hailey asked. "But I was going to show your teacher. When she comes in, I'll announce you like: *Drumroll, please . . . introducing the top junior soloist of the nation: Harper!"*

Hailey proceeded to fangirl around me, jumping around and squealing and acting like she was going to faint.

"Hailey, you're amazing, but that's enough!" I said. Someone might come in the room and see this! What if that someone was Miss Vanessa? Or other people auditioning? I didn't want anyone to think I brought my trophy—and my own crazed superfan—with me! *Uh, Mom? A little help here?* Where was that dance mom now that I needed her?

"I can't believe I'm in the same room as Harper!" Hailey was enjoying this way too much. "I luuuuurve you!"

I did what I had to do to get Hailey out of here. For some reason, Hailey hated hugs. So I grabbed her and squeezed her super tight into a bear hug.

"I luuuurve you too," I said.

"Ack! You're squashing me! Let me go!"

"Only if you take that trophy back to the car," I said.

The door opened and I gasped. Fortunately, it was just my mother.

"Hailey, where did you go? Are you two wrestling? And can you tell me why you wanted to bring Harper's trophy in here?" my mom asked. "You know what, I don't even want to know anymore."

"Mom, we gotta go back to the car! Quick!" Hailey said. I loosened my grip, and Hailey picked up the trophy and raced out the door.

So sweet. But so potentially embarrassing.

I sat down on the floor and did some leg stretches. The door opened again, and this time a girl came in. She had her black hair in a bun at the nape of her neck and was wearing a black halter-style leotard. She was looking at her phone and didn't see me.

"11:11," she said to herself.

"Make a wish!" I blurted out. I would have felt stupid about eavesdropping, except the girl said, "Make a wish!" exactly the same time I did. We both laughed.

"Close your eyes," the girl said.

I closed my eyes. Of course my wish was that my audition would go well and I'd make the competition team. When I opened my eyes, the girl was opening hers, too.

"Hope our wishes come true," I said.

"Me too," the girl said. "Sorry to barge in on you, by the way. They told me to come and cool down from my audition. Oh, just so you know? The audition's not too bad."

I let out a big sigh of relief.

The door opened again.

"Harper, Vanessa is ready for you."

*W*elcome to DanceStarz, Harper."

Vanessa was younger than the owner of my dance studio in Connecticut. She had very light, short, slicked-back blond hair and stood with a dancer's posture.

I smiled at her, in my own best dance posture, showing I was confident, cool, and in control.

"Hanks," I squeaked. *Hanks? HANKS? So much for trying to seem confident, cool, and in control.* I tried again. "I mean, hello! Thanks!"

Definitely not so confident, cool, or in control. Great way to make a first impression. My nerves were even worse than I'd thought they'd be. Vanessa was intimidating.

"As you know, you missed the official competition auditions, but we're making an exception for you and another member," Vanessa said. "You both have strong recommendations from your former teachers and a nice track record at competitions."

Really intimidating.

Sure, I'd been judged a million times at competitions. But I'd never had to be evaluated to be a part of a dance studio. In Connecticut, my teachers had watched me grow up there and knew where I was supposed to be placed. This felt like my whole life was being evaluated. What if I'd lost my dance skills since I'd moved? What if they'd disappeared, like my old house and my old life had? I suddenly pictured myself trying to dance for Vanessa and freezing like a statue. Or falling on my butt. Or passing out. Or vomiting.

"Let's see you dance," she said.

I took a deep breath and got ready.

Vanessa ran me through a warm-up, and went through the five basic positions of ballet, which were as natural to me as breathing. My mind might be blurry, but my muscle memory kicked in.

"You have a natural turnout." Vanessa nodded.

In real life, people usually aren't going around checking out your feet, unless maybe you're wearing cute flip-flops or have a great pedicure. But in dance, your feet are judged. I was lucky to have a natural turnout—or what my dance teachers called "good feet."

But other things I'd be judged on weren't about luck.

Next up were splits: right, left, and straddle.

Vanessa nodded. She put on some upbeat, jazzy music. "Let's start with some leaps. How about a jeté?"

I went to one of the far corners of the floor.

I used all of my strength and sprang into the air as my legs split, hoping to impress Miss Vanessa. I glanced over to see her reaction, but her expression simply looked thoughtful. She wasn't giving anything away.

Next, I did a switch leap. I brought my left leg forward, to show I was just as good on both sides.

"A turn series, please," Vanessa said. The pirouette is one of the most difficult of all of the dance steps. You spin around on one foot, with your raised foot touching your knee. My pirouettes had been my shining move, and I'd worked all summer in my room perfecting my turn series of pirouettes so I could do even more in a row. I felt a surge of excitement to show Vanessa what I could do.

I took my prep and held my plié for a second, making sure my technique was perfect, then pulled up spotting seven consecutive turns with a graceful landing. *YES!*

Nailed it.

"Let's do a new combination," Vanessa said. "We won't do the whole thirty-two-beat combination."

I followed her directions and did the combo. Vanessa asked me to make some corrections. I reminded myself not to panic that I'd done them poorly, as she might have been seeing how well I took direction. I did the best I could.

"Now let's see your tumbling skills."

Okay. I wasn't the best tumbler on my old team by far, but I could do the basics and a little bit more.

First, I did a cartwheel. Then a back bend. Then a back walkover and back handspring and some not-too-bad hand walks.

"Can you do an aerial?" Vanessa asked me.

"No." I was honest. "I'm working on it, though. I definitely want to take a tumbling class."

"Okay. Now please show me the prepared piece you brought," Vanessa said.

I took a deep breath. This was my favorite dance I'd ever competed with, and I wanted to do it for her perfectly.

"It's my solo from the last nationals," I told her. "It's a lyrical piece."

Vanessa cued up the music I had sent her ahead of time.

I started in second position. I leaned forward with my head slightly lowered and fluttered my arms up. And then the music began.

I lost myself in the dance. I forgot where I was. I heard the music, let it flow through my body as I danced. I did my grand finale, my signature turn series: seven pirouettes into a kick spin.

"Clean lines." Vanessa nodded. "Nice technique."

"Thank you," I said, breathless but feeling pretty exhilarated.

"Harper," Vanessa said. "How do you feel when you dance?"

"It's fun," I said. Weak. I would need to do better than that.

I took a deep breath and started again. "I feel so focused when I'm dancing. It's like I can turn off my brain and my body just can flow. I love it."

"And you would be up for the commitment a competition team requires?" she asked.

"Definitely," I said without hesitation.

"Check your e-mail tonight for your placement," Vanessa said. "Welcome to DanceStarz."

To: HarperDancer

From: DanceStarz Academy

Congratulations! After careful consideration, we are pleased to invite you to be a member of:

DanceStarz Squad

DanceStarz Squad is our select competition team.

We believe this is a special honor, as you will be representing DanceStarz in our very first ever junior select competition team.

We look forward to seeing you at the studio.

YESSSS

YESSSSSSSSSS

YESSSSSSSSSSSSSSSSSSSSSSSSSSSSSSSSSSSSSSSSSS!!

4

'm someone who likes to be punctual, and usually even early. For the first day of competition team, I made sure to get there extra early. I laid out my outfit the night before, even though it was just basic dance clothes. I chose a lavender dance top with crisscross straps and black compression shorts. Sleek and clean, but not too showy. I wanted to lie low at first.

I obviously wasn't the only person to have the idea of getting there early. When I walked into Studio A, three girls were already in there, taking a selfie against the black wall. They looked up as I approached them.

"Hi! I'm Harper," I said, and smiled.

The girls all looked me up and down.

"Harper. Huh," one girl said.

"This is the select competition team," the girl in the middle of the three jumped in. She had dark brown hair in braids and was wearing a black high-necked mesh top and black dance shorts. "You're probably supposed to be in Studio B."

They continued to take selfies.

"Actually, I'm supposed to be here. I'm on the select team," I explained.

The girls looked at each other. The middle girl spoke again. "Do we know you?"

"No, I'm new. I just moved here from Connecticut," I said.

None of the girls said anything. Awkward.

"Wow, that's so weird," another girl finally said. "Vanessa didn't tell us there would be any new people on the team. We thought it was going to be people we knew. You weren't at the open auditions."

"I missed those because I just moved here," I said. "I did an individual audition instead."

I waited for them to introduce themselves. But they just went back to taking selfies. Obviously, I was dismissed. I tried to look busy by taking my duffel bag to the cubbies and finding an empty one near the bottom. I hoped there were going to be more people on the team.

My wish was granted! Another girl walked in, with a big smile—the same friendly girl I'd seen on audition day. She had her black hair up in a high pony and was wearing a teal wrap top with teal, black, and white patterned dance shorts.

The other girls gave her the same confused look they'd given me earlier. Her smile faltered. I remembered how she had made me feel better when I'd been nervous at the audition. I needed to return that favor.

"Hi!" I said, walking over. "Remember me from the auditions? I'm Harper."

"Yes! We made the wish together. I'm Lily." She smiled at everyone.

The door opened again and Vanessa entered. Everyone fell silent and, I noticed, straightened up.

"Congratulations, everyone!" Vanessa said. "You are the five members of DanceStarz's first select junior competition team: DanceStarz Squad."

Everyone clapped.

"The Squad!" A girl with black curls let out a cheer.

"Vanessa? Is this everyone?" the girl in the black top asked.

"Yes." Vanessa nodded. "We're going to start small but mighty. You five dancers were purposefully selected."

"But what about—?"

"See me after class for further questions," Vanessa shut her down. "Let's warm up and I'll share a little more about the team."

Everyone found a spot on the floor. Vanessa walked us through isolations and crunches and push-ups. Everyone stayed very focused. After we warmed up, Vanessa gathered us around so we could sit in a circle.

"Let me introduce myself," Vanessa said. "For those of you who don't know me, I was a professional dancer on and off Broadway until last year. I was also a competitive dancer here in Florida since I was five. I was brought in to DanceStarz to take over the competition teams and will be taking things in a new direction here." She smiled.

Everyone nodded approvingly. That was cool.

"This team is the first select team," Vanessa said. "You are some of the most advanced dancers in this studio and the community. I know you're all in middle school, but I am going to push you—because I want you to do your best and *be* your best."

We all nodded.

"Let's have you introduce yourselves," Vanessa said. "Why don't you tell us your favorite dance style and your favorite color? Then demonstrate for us something that showcases you. Who would—?"

The girl with the dark hair in braids shot up her hand.

"Megan." Vanessa nodded and the girl jumped up and stood in front of us with confidence.

"Hi, I'm Megan Snow! I love contemporary dance and my favorite color is gold. Except at competitions, when it's platinum."

Platinum is often the highest award. We all laughed.

"And now my move," Megan said. She raised her left leg through passé. It was super impressive. She didn't even use her hands to hold it, just her leg muscles. Then she did a needle. Then she lay down with her chin on the floor and pulled her legs back over her head—and rolled over. Twice!

Whoa. Megan was seriously flexible. And confident. She was going to be a hard act to follow. Everyone clapped.

A girl with wavy reddish-blond hair in a high ponytail stood up. She was wearing a coral halter top and coral-and-black-patterned shorts.

"My name is Riley Rosen, and I love hot pink and hip-hop."

Riley did some really cool isolation moves and finished in a split, with super facial expressions. She was definitely confident—a *performer.* More claps for Riley.

The girl with curly black hair, wearing a white lace top and black leggings, walked to the middle of the floor.

"Hi, I'm Trina Uba, and I love all colors, so my favorite is rainbow. And my favorite dance is tap."

Trina flew into a quick combination. She was shuffling and doing time steps so fast it was like her feet were separate from her body. I couldn't believe how quickly her feet tapped through the movements. Her footwork was insane to me. Many claps.

Lily was up next.

"Hey, my name is Lily Hu. Obviously, I'm new here. I love turquoise and tumbling, so my favorite dance style is acro."

Lily went over to grab a tumbling mat. She put her hands over her head. She did a back handspring. Then she did a round-off/handspring/tuck, her long black hair flying out behind her. Next she did a round-off handspring stepout and two aerials in a row, with perfectly stuck landings. And finally she did a back tuck like it was nothing.

Whoa. I saw why acro was her favorite style. Her tricks were incredible. I clapped like crazy.

Then it was my turn. My big chance to maybe impress the girls and Vanessa.

"Hi, I'm Harper McCoy. I love purple, and my favorite dance is lyrical."

I had decided to show off my turns. I hoped my pirouettes that had impressed everyone back in Connecticut would be slightly impressive here. I went to the center of the room and stood in fourth position. I fixed my gaze on a spot at eye level. Then I bent both legs into a deep plié, held my arms in first position and then: I sprang up! I spun around and around. And around . . .

One . . . two . . . three . . . four . . . five . . . SIX! SEVEN!

Up until that point, everything was going great, but then my nerves got the best of me. I did a leg hold turn and tried to stop on a relevé—but I didn't control it and I wobbled the ending.

Ugh.

Everyone clapped, and I could hear Lily call out: "Whoo!"

I sat down and joined the group, face flushed. I'd done okay, but I'd wanted to be perfect and really show my technique and nail it. I'd wanted to prove why I should be here. I wasn't sure if I had.

"Bravo to all of you," Vanessa said. "And now you all have an inkling of why you've been chosen for the elite team. Next time, we'll start putting all of this together. There will be mandatory classes and optional classes. Ballet twice a week—"

Riley groaned loudly.

"Yes, twice," Vanessa said firmly. "Ballet is the foundation for the all of the other dances."

I knew Riley wasn't alone in this thinking. I saw Lily give Riley a little nod. Some of my dance friends found ballet boring or just too hard. I actually liked ballet. It was a challenge, getting everything precise and right. And when you did, it was beautiful.

"As you know, DanceStarz already has competition teams," Vanessa said. "But I was brought in to expand the program. As the first select team, it's going to take a lot of commitment. I will need one hundred percent dedication from each of you. But I think you're up for the task."

Everyone nodded.

Vanessa continued. "I'll be ordering official team warm-ups for us to wear to the competitions. And speaking of, our very first competition will be a bit later in the season, so we can focus on becoming a team and getting to know each other. And, of course, starting to figure out a routine!"

Everyone applauded, but I shuddered a little inside. Performing was the goal—but also scary.

"Will there be solos?" Megan asked. Apparently, not all of us were scared.

"Eventually, there will be solos and duets and trios," Vanessa said. "But first, team dances. I want us to become a *team*. And as you know, there's no *I* in team!"

"But there's 'me' in 'team,'" Trina said. The other girls looked at her. "*M* and *E*? *T* . . . *E* . . . *A* . . . *M*?"

Everybody giggled.

"We'll begin learning our first team routine at our next rehearsal," Vanessa said, bypassing Trina's comment. "And now, team announcements. Your team jackets will be arriving next week."

Everyone cheered! Team jackets were a big deal.

"I want to know what they look like!" Riley yelled.

"Still a secret." Vanessa smiled. "We will have the big reveal when they arrive."

We all groaned. I knew we were all dying of suspense.

"Moving on. As you know, DanceStarz will be marching in the annual town parade this weekend."

I had seen that on the website, but the sign-up date had passed before we moved here. I'd been disappointed, because parades can be really fun.

"Lily and Harper, you may still sign up and be a part of it," she continued. "I would like all of DanceStarz Squad represented. Ask at the front desk for a permission form."

Lily and I grinned at each other.

"Any questions before you're dismissed?" Vanessa asked.

Megan raised her hand. "Can we do our ritual?"

"Certainly," Vanessa said.

Megan, Riley, and Trina jumped up together.

"Ring, ring!" They started by holding their hands up like they were ringing a bell.

"Ring, ring! Tap, tap, pat, pat!" They tapped their noses and patted their knees.

Lily and I just stood there, waiting until they were finished. They let out a cheer and a laugh.

"Obviously, if you are going to continue that tradition, you'll have to explain the significance and teach that to the new girls," Vanessa said.

"Oh!" Megan said innocently. "Of course."

*egan, Riley, and Trina left immediately together, and Lily followed out the door. I was the last one to leave because, for some reason, my duffel bag wasn't where I'd left it. I finally found it tucked into a corner. I found a navy T-shirt and a denim skirt, and I pulled them over my dance clothes and changed my dance shoes for flip-flops. When I entered the lobby, it was hectic.

"Oops!" I almost tripped over a toddler in a pale pink leotard and tutu. Adorable. Parents and little kids in leotards or dance tops and shorts were milling around. This was what I was used to: a busy dance studio.

"Harper!" Lily came running up to me. "My parents own

the frozen yogurt place in this plaza. Do you want to come with me and check it out?"

"Okay!"

Cool! That perked me up. It would be nice to get to know Lily better. I felt like we had a lot in common: being the new girls, starting at a new studio, and, of course, we loved dance.

I looked around for Mom and spotted her sitting on one of the chairs in front of the TV, watching a split screen of a tap class and hip-hop class simultaneously. It was so cool to see all the younger dancers, boys and girls, doing their thing.

"Mom, can I walk over to the frozen yogurt place with Lily?" I asked. "Her parents own it, so they'll be there."

"Harper!" Mom turned and smiled. Then she looked at the women on the couch across from her.

"Hello," the women all said to me.

"Oh, sorry," I said. "I didn't mean to interrupt. I thought my mom was looking at the TV."

"Oh, we were," a mom said. She looked like a grown-up replica of Megan.

"I was telling your mother how Studio A is on the bigger portion of the screen. Since you girls are the top dancers of the studio, the best of the best, you will usually be on that screen."

"Oh." I wasn't quite sure how to respond to that one.

"This is quite a team you're joining, I think you should know," Megan's mom said. "Megan alone has won endless titles and awards, like Miss FutureStar and hall of fame and top ten and—"

"And Riley has won Miss ShowBiz and Junior Miss Energy and—" Riley's mom jumped in.

"Wow!" my mom said.

"Riley, Megan, and Trina have been dancing together since they were toddlers," Megan's mother said.

"Dance runs in our blood!" Riley's mom said. "Megan's mother and I danced together on the high school dance team. She was our dance team leader and led us to states three years in a row."

"Those were the good old days." Megan's mother smiled.

"Dance is our life." Riley's mother nodded, doing a little salsa move in her chair.

"Oh, we could reminisce all day," Megan's mother said. "But I know Harper is anxious to know my Megan and the other girls better. Tell Megan she has permission to go get yogurt with you too."

Oh.

Not that I wouldn't have invited the other girls, but I wasn't sure what Lily was thinking, and she hadn't mentioned anyone else. And I definitely wasn't sure the other girls would even want to go with us. I looked over at the trio, who had put on summer dresses over their dance clothes. They were surrounded by a group of younger girls who looked dressed for hip-hop class in tank tops, sweats, and a few knit and baseball hats.

"Riley may go too, then. We have to stick around anyway, since Riley's little sister has hip-hop next." Riley's mom tilted her head at the hip-hop dancers. Then she hissed, "Quinn! Get to class!"

The hip-hop dancers scattered.

"Well, your sister looks occupied," my mother said, waving toward Hailey sitting on a chair with her tablet, oblivious. "So I'll bring her over in a half hour. I'm sure she'd like some frozen yogurt too."

"Thanks, Mom!" I said, and I looked around for Lily.

One of the younger dancers, who had just come out of the hip-hop class, tapped me on the shoulder.

"Excuse me, did you come out of the room with the Bunheads?" she asked me. "Are you on the new competition team?"

"Yeah!" I said proudly. "I am on the team."

"That's so cool. I want to be on the Squad when I'm older," the girl said excitedly. "I wanted to say congratulations."

That was really nice. I thanked her. I'd always looked up

to the older girls on the top teams in my old studio, so it was really cool to be the one who kids looked up to now.

Although I wondered what she meant by the Bunheads? Maybe that was our unofficial nickname?

I went over to Lily.

"Sooo," I said hesitantly. "My mom said yes. Also, the other moms were there and they heard me. Is it okay if the other girls come too?"

"Do they even want to come?" Lily asked.

"I know, right?" I said, relieved. I was a little glad I wasn't the only one feeling slightly snubbed. "I guess we could ask them and find out."

"You go first," Lily said, with a little nervous laugh.

Fabulous.

"Hi," I said to the trio. They didn't respond. "Excuse me, hi!"

"Hi!" Trina turned around with a grin.

"I wanted to invite you guys to the frozen yogurt place with Lily and me," I said. "So we can get to know each other now that we're all Bunheads."

The trio looked at each other. Riley started laughing.

"No offense," Megan said. "But *we're* not all Bunheads. Bunheads is just me, Riley, and Trina. Ever since we all started in pre-K ballet."

"Oh." I laughed, super uncomfortable. "Ha. I thought it was the nickname for our team."

"No," Riley said. "Just the three of us."

Awkward silence.

"Anyway!" I cleared my throat. "Do you guys want to go to the frozen yogurt place with Lily and me?" Also known as the Not-Bunheads, apparently.

"Ah." Megan wrinkled her nose. "I'd love to, but I have to go to an appointment at the . . . uh . . ."

Yeah, yeah, I knew where this was going. I considered playing along with it so I could get to know Lily first before trying to break into the Bunhead world. But the mothers were all looking at us.

"Actually, Megan," I interrupted, "your mother already said yes, so I guess your appointment is canceled."

Megan rolled her eyes.

"You asked my mother? Fine. We'll go. But first I need to talk to Miss Vanessa." Megan went off to the front desk.

"Ooh, I can go." Trina was looking at her phone. "My sister says she can pick me up later."

"You have a sister who drives?" I asked.

Trina nodded. "She's a senior in high school."

"She's a cheerleader and she's really cool," Riley said.

"Trina is so lucky. I only have an annoying little sister."

"I've got one of those and an annoying older brother," I said. "But he's at college, so he's less annoying—except when he comes home for break and I'll have to move into Hailey's bedroom."

"I'm an only child," Lily said. "So I think you're all lucky."

"Well, *you're* lucky because your parents own a frozen yogurt place!" I said.

"Your parents own it?" Trina said. "Oh, cool! I'm excited to try it."

"Yeah, before this, we had nowhere to walk to except, like, a vacuum store," Riley said.

"I mean, it was sometimes fun to go see the different vacuums," Trina said. Nobody responded and Trina looked at them. "What? Nobody else likes to look at vacuums? With their cute hoses?"

"Um . . . no. Just no," Riley told her.

"Oh. Well, I hope there's cookies-and-cream fro-yo. That's my favorite!" Trina said, just as Megan returned. *Uh-oh.* Megan looked furious.

"You okay?" Riley asked her.

"Let's just go," Megan said angrily. I had no choice but to follow her out the door. They walked along the sidewalk, the

Bunheads in the lead and Lily and me trailing behind.

"Just FYI, I'm not a huge fan of fro-yo," Megan grumbled as they walked past the vacuum place.

"We also have smoothies," Lily responded. She did a cartwheel and bounced up.

"Megan *loves* smoothies!" Trina said.

I glanced over to see if Megan was softening up, but obviously something was still putting her in a bad mood.

"Is everything okay?" I asked her tentatively.

"No, actually it's not," Megan spat. "It's about Isabelle and Bella. The Bells."

Riley and Trina started making the hand motion of ringing the bells, like they had in their closing ritual in class.

Megan shot them a look and they stopped.

"The Bells made that up," Trina explained to us.

"I thought Isabelle and Bella would be here on our team," Megan continued. "Vanessa just said the five we have are the right fit. What's that supposed to mean?"

"We always fit together." Riley frowned. "They're the Bells; we're the Bunheads!"

"We've always been on the same team, since we were all minis!" Trina looked puzzled.

"My trios with them won first place last year." Megan

looked upset. "I finally got to do trios with them instead of just them doing duos. And now they're gone."

"Oh my gosh." Trina gasped. "Do you think they didn't make the team?"

"Wait just one second," Riley said. "Do you think Vanessa replaced them with . . ."

The Bunheads all turned slowly and looked at Lily and me. And none of them looked happy. Lily shot me a panicked look. Were these girls going to hold us responsible for their friends not being on the team?

Megan's phone made an alert noise.

"Well, maybe we'll get some answers. Isabelle just posted a video." Megan looked at her phone. Then she gasped and stopped walking.

"What?" Riley asked her.

Megan stuck her hand out so Riley could see her phone. Trina peeked over her shoulder. I casually tried to get a look too, but my view was blocked. Riley and Trina both literally screamed.

I needed to know.

"What is it?" I asked.

If Megan looked furious before, she looked even more so now.

"Isabelle and Bella joined Energii," she practically hissed.

"WHAT?" Riley looked like she was going to throw up.

"What's Energii?" Lily asked.

Megan held out her phone to us. There was an image of two girls wearing white leotards with orange and yellow star-bursts on them. The caption said:

Welcome to Energii, Isabelle James and Bella Martinez!

I'd heard of Energii. When my mom was looking at dance studios to join, she had mentioned it. She'd said it was too far to be convenient and too big.

"They've been around forever," Riley told us. "They're way bigger than DanceStarz."

"They win all the time," Trina added glumly. "Look how many 'likes' they have too."

"And they're our major rivals," Megan said. She looked really upset.

Ouch. I understood how hard that was. It was bad enough to compete against your friends. But to have them at a rival studio—now, that was really going to be hard.

"Sorry," I said. "That's a shocker."

"Those traitors," Megan said. "How could they join Energii?"

"They probably signed up," Trina said knowingly.

"I *know* they signed up," Megan said to her. "I mean why? How could they join our rivals?"

"Well, if they didn't make our select team, they were probably upset," Riley said.

"That's it," Megan nodded. "They joined for revenge."

"And now we have to try to beat them," Riley said.

"We beat them by training hard now and doing things they can't do!" I gave a pep talk. The Bunheads were nodding.

"Yes," Trina nodded solemnly.

"Do you think they're mad at us?" Riley asked Megan. "Are they mad at you?"

Megan stuck her phone in her pocket and looked at Riley. "Let's talk about this later. *In private.*"

I guessed this wasn't going to be the last I would hear about Isabelle and Bella. But for now, I was glad to change the subject. "Maybe frozen yogurt will help your mood." I started walking again and, fortunately, they followed me to the fro-yo store.

"Okay!" Lily perked up. "This is my family's new store."

She pushed open the door, which said:

SUGAR PLUMS

"Oh, it's so *cute*!" Trina clapped her hands.

It was!

The walls were seafoam and ice blue, and colored stools were set at white round tables and long high-top tables. There were two other customers at a round table, and a man and a woman behind the counter. Along the back wall were lots of stations where you could choose your own fro-yo flavor—my favorite, since I like being able to mix up the flavors I want!

"Welcome to Sugar Plums!" the man behind the counter said.

"Dad, this is my new dance team." Lily introduced us all.

"Very happy to meet everyone." Lily's father smiled widely. "Your first treat is on the house!"

"Thank you!" we all said. *Awesome!*

Megan leaned into the counter, nudging me out of the way.

"Are the mangos very fresh?" Megan asked. When Lily's father said they were, Megan ordered a large mango smoothie.

"And I'll have a smoothie too," Riley said. "Banana berry blast, please."

As the blender buzzed with the smoothies, I took one of the yogurt cups. Lily and Trina and I went over to the handles in the wall.

"Chocolate, white chocolate, and chocolate mint," Lily announced. "Yes, I'm chocolate obsessed."

"I'm going to get half cheesecake and half birthday cake," Trina said.

"A cake theme! Very festive," I said. I decided on original tart and the July flavor of the month, blueberry. I loved blueberries. I pulled the handle slowly and filled my cup with two-thirds original and one-third blueberry.

"AH!" Trina yelped. "I'm out of control!"

Trina's cup was practically overflowing.

"Push the handle!" Lily said to her, laughing.

"Good thing I really like cheesecake," Trina said, looking at her giant yogurt.

"Don't worry, that happens until you get the hang of it," Lily's father called over to us.

Trina basically stuck her face in her cup and bit off the top of the yogurt swirl, saving the yogurt from toppling over.

"AH! Brain freeze!" she yelped again.

Everyone in the store was cracking up, even Megan and Riley. I hoped everyone would stay in this happier mood. I took my yogurt up to the counter, and Lily's mom topped it at my request with blueberries and whipped cream. Lily got hers topped with hot fudge sauce and cookie crumbles. Trina got sprinkles in her "favorite color"—rainbow.

We all sat down on stools at a high-top table. Lily's father came over to check on us.

"My smoothie is very good, Lily's Dad!" Megan called out.

Lily's father smiled back at her. I had a feeling Megan was very good at charming parents.

"Tell your friends about us," he said. "We hope to have Sugar Plums dancing all over Florida."

"Ohhh," I said. "Did you name the shop after the Sugar Plum Fairy from *The Nutcracker*?"

"Yes!" Lily's father answered. "We named it after our dancer: Lily was the Sugar Plum Fairy in her last ballet performance. Well, enjoy!"

Lily looked embarrassed as her father beamed with pride. He went back behind the counter.

"I love the Sugar Plum Fairy," Trina said. "It's such a beautiful role."

"You must be really good," I added. The Sugar Plum Fairy's solo is one of the most famous solos for a ballerina. "How long have you been dancing?"

"I've danced ballet since I was three," Lily said. "My studio was ballet-focused and not competitive, so this is really different for me. My parents are really into ballet."

"Why didn't you go to the ballet studio, then?" Riley asked.

"I actually like tumbling best, and competitions sound fun," Lily said. "And when my parents bought the store here, they had to admit it made sense for me to try DanceStarz."

"How long have you all been at DanceStarz?" I asked the other girls.

"Well, it's only been open for three years. But I was the very first person to sign up," Megan said. "I'm the original."

"I was second!" Riley interjected. "My mom was with her mom."

"We've been dancing at Miss Lucille's since we were three," Megan said. "But DanceStarz opened up right here, so my mother made us switch. So it's cool. I've won two national titles and have been top five, top ten, so many times."

"And a lot of photogenic awards," Riley added.

Megan flashed us a winning smile.

"What about you?" Trina asked.

"I've been at the same studio in Connecticut since I was four," I told her.

"Near New York City, right?" Megan asked.

"Yeah, we'd take the train into the city sometimes." I smiled just thinking about some of the great memories I had with my team. "Our team went on field trips to Broadway shows, we saw the Rockettes, did a workshop with American Ballet Company—"

"Wow, you're in for major disappointment here," Megan interrupted, and rolled her eyes.

"Oh, no! I didn't mean that," I protested. "I heard Florida has an incredible dance culture. Also, you guys have fun stuff here I didn't have at home. Like all the pools. Our neighborhood has a pool, if you guys want to come over."

"Oh my gosh, Trina has the *best* pool at her house," Riley said. "It's an infinity pool with a diving board and a slide. We practice our leaps off the diving board. Remember that time . . . ?"

The Bunheads started reminiscing about their great times at Trina's pool, which sounded like it blew our neighborhood pool out of the water. Well, I liked our neighborhood pool. We'd never had one in Connecticut except the town pool, so that was one upgrade. I ate a spoonful of my frozen yogurt quietly.

It was delicious, but I had a sour taste in my mouth. It was going to be a challenge to be on a team made up of BFFs. Maybe we'd bond more after we'd competed. Or been in a parade together. I waited until there was a break in the conversation.

"So, what about this parade?" I jumped in.

"It's the town anniversary parade," Riley said. "We march in it every year."

"So fun," I said. "My old dance team marched in a couple parades too—"

"In New York City?" Megan asked.

"Actually, yes!" I perked up. "Once. My team marched in a Veterans Day parade down the streets in the middle of Manhattan. It was really exciting."

"You're going to be majorly disappointed," Megan said again. "This is, like, a small parade."

"I didn't mean I was comparing," I backtracked. "I'm sure it's going to be fun."

"Meh." Megan shrugged. "It's, like, the school marching band, little baseball teams, scout troops. That kind of thing."

"My sister's squad is cheering," Trina added.

"Her sister's an amazing cheerleader," Riley said.

Speaking of sisters . . .

"Ha!" Megan suddenly laughed. "Look at that kid."

I casually looked over and almost choked on my frozen yogurt. My sister had her face pressed up against the window, her nose squashed like a pig's. She crossed her eyes and made a googly face at us.

I sighed.

Hailey came into the shop and right up to our table.

"Aren't you precious," Megan said to her. "How old are you?"

"I'm eight," Hailey said, and then got distracted by the huge topping bar. "Ooh! They have gummy bears."

"Go get a yogurt," I told her. "Be careful when pulling the handle."

Hailey skipped off toward the cups.

"My sister's eight too," Riley said. "Quinn is on the minis team. Is Hailey going to take dance too?"

"Not yet." I shook my head. "She does take dance sometimes, but usually only once a week. My mom wanted to see if I liked DanceStarz before she had Hailey do anything at the studio."

"Do you?" Megan leaned in. "Do you like DanceStarz?"

The Bunheads looked at me expectantly.

I suddenly felt like they wanted me to say no, I hated it and was quitting. And that maybe if I quit, one of their old Bell friends would come back and take my place on the team.

"Do I like DanceStarz? Yes," I said firmly. "And I can't wait for our team to dance."

6

$\mathcal{M}$om and I were looking at dance websites to get some new black shorts for the parade and a few more things for practice. New clothes always cheered me up a little.

I was sitting in the living room with Mom, Hailey, and Mo. Mo was our Yorkie. He was black and brown, fluffy and adorable. Right now, he was sleeping in the patch of sun next to the window. Hailey was on a window seat playing a game on her tablet.

Like the studio, our new house was brighter and airier than our old house. It was all on one floor and had a screened-in porch, floor-to-ceiling windows, and everything in it was white or bleached wood. It was cheerful, although I wasn't sure I was cheerful about being there. Maybe I just needed to get used to my new home. I liked the vibe, and my mom was letting me help her decorate it slowly (especially with lots of furry pillows).

"Let's get you some new tops, too," Mom said. "Buy one, get one free."

Ooh! I chose one with wide crisscross straps going up and down the back.

"Which color? There's emerald, hot pink, citron, and eggplant."

"Eggplant," I said, even though I noticed the other girls here tended toward bright colors. The bright ones were super cute and fun, but for some reason I gravitated toward wearing black or pretty, low-key colors. Then I chose a flowy black tank top that had strings that tied up the back.

"Thanks, Mom." I gave her a hug.

"Dad's home!" Dad called out like he always did when he came home from work. He came in and kissed Mom and me on our heads. "Harper, how was the dance studio?"

"Good? I think?" I wasn't totally sure yet. "I'll know more when I start classes."

"It's hard starting somewhere new," Mom said. "I met

some of the other mothers. Their daughters have been dancing together since they were little."

My mom had been the team mom last year and used to work behind the front desk helping with the bookkeeping at my old studio. She had known all the other moms for years too. I hadn't thought about how she might be missing her people, as well.

"It's an adjustment for all of us," Dad said. "We have to look for the good parts."

"There's one other new girl, Lily, who seems really nice," I said. "Her parents own the frozen yogurt place near the dance studio."

"They have good frozen yogurt in Florida." Hailey nodded happily. "They let me put on so many gummies I feel sick."

"Oh," my mother said. "Wonderful."

"Oh, but also," I said, "everyone did compliment me on my pirouettes."

"Well, they should!" Hailey was indignant.

"Well, the other girls are really talented," I said. "Huge handsprings, back tucks, crazy good performance skills, and the fastest tap dancing I ever saw."

"That's good," Dad said. "You want to surround yourself with the best so you can learn from them."

"And so your team can win competitions," Mom added.

"On the bad side, if everyone else is really good, then you could be the worst one and make everyone lose," Hailey said.

"Hailey!" Mom admonished her.

But that was exactly what I had been thinking. What if I was the weak link?

"Whose turn is it to take the dog out?" Mom asked.

"Jack's!" Hailey said, joking. Jack was our older brother. He went to college back in Connecticut and had decided to stay up there for summer classes. Although he'd already gone there for a year, it was a little weird that he couldn't just get in his car and come home anytime he wanted to do laundry anymore. But, it also meant that I was the oldest sibling in our house. So, I was kind of the boss!

"Hailey's!" I said, jumping up. "Sorry, I have to go watch my show!"

"No fair!" Hailey whined.

"I'll do it tomorrow when your singing show is on," I made a deal with her.

I gave my mom another thank-you hug for the mini shopping spree and headed upstairs. Yay, my show was on! I liked all the shows that had dancers on, but this one where kids competed against one another with professional dancers was the one I made sure to watch live so I didn't get any spoilers.

I went into my bedroom. I'd spent the last two weeks since we'd moved in setting it up, and I was pretty happy with how it had turned out. The walls were white and my bedding was white with deep purple fluffy pillows on it. I had a lavender chair and some of my stuffed animals on the bed.

My parents had put up shelves for things I brought home from dance competitions: all kinds of trophies, medals, and other kinds of plaques. On a large bulletin board, I'd hung my ribbons and pendants and thumbtacked up my special award certificates:

Excellence in Technique

Best Precision

Synchronized Prize

I also had a bookshelf for my favorite books and framed pictures of my friends from my old dance team and from school. In my closet, along with my regular clothes, were my old costumes. I couldn't bear to part with any of them. Hanging on the closet door were all the headbands, ribbons, and bows. It was definitely the room of someone who liked to dance! And someone who was an organization queen, with everything neatly folded, stacked, and tucked into its proper place.

I'd kept a corner of my room empty so I could stretch and even dance a bit.

I set my laptop up on the floor, angled so I could see the screen as I stretched. I had voted for my favorite dancer, so I was hoping she wouldn't get sent home tonight. I heard a scratching noise at the door. I got up to let Mo in—and behind him was Hailey.

"Can I watch it with you, please?" Hailey begged.

Sigh. I liked to watch my show alone and really focus on the dance moves. But I knew my sister hadn't had the chance to make any new friends yet and was lonely.

"Okay, come on in," I said. "The judges just gave harsh critiques to my favorite dancer, so I'm scared."

We sat down on the floor and watched together, Mo included. I used my foot stretcher on each foot while I watched the performers do dance moves I dreamed of doing someday.

"The boy should win," Hailey said.

"Don't you disrespect my favorite!" I said. "Mo, am I right or am I right?"

Mo inched closer to the screen and rolled over.

"He wants to be on the show." Hailey laughed. "We have to teach him to dance! I'll be right back."

"Do you want to be a dancer?" I scratched Mo's tummy, and he leaned into me as if to say, yes, he did. Or, to be honest, *Yes, whatever you say as long as you keep scratching me.*

Hailey came back in holding a bag of dog treats. Mo stood up on his back legs and tried to get the treats.

"Dance!" Hailey commanded. "Harper, show Mo what to do. Do a twirl."

I stood up and did some turns. Hailey circled her hand around, so Mo would get the idea. Mo stood on his back paws! He was going to dance!

"AOOOOoooo!" Mo howled.

Hailey and I both cracked up, hysterical.

"AooOOOO!"

"Not *sing*! Dance!" I said, clutching my side from laughing. "I'm dead."

"I guess Mo is a singer like me. He can go on a singing show instead." Hailey shrugged, giggling. "High five, Mo."

Hailey held up her hand to high-five. Mo licked it instead. We started laughing again. Hailey gave up and gave Mo a treat, which he ate and then promptly lay down and fell asleep.

"Well, dancing *is* hard work." I laughed. "It can wear you out. But, Mo, you can't give up so quickly; it takes a lot of practice."

Like I needed to do. I sat back down and got out the foot stretcher again.

would be taking two kinds of classes. Some classes were just for our competition team, with the five of us. They would help us learn our routines and other skills we would need for competition. The other kind were classes that were open to other dancers at the advanced level. These dancers might be on the younger competition team, or prepping to make our team someday, hopefully.

Today, I would be taking my first class with dancers not on my team. It was a lyrical class for the intermediate/ advanced level.

As I walked in, I saw there were about fifteen girls and boys all stretching, talking, and getting ready for class. A couple people turned and looked at me. One younger girl whispered to another loud enough for me to hear: "She made the Squad."

I gave them a little smile. I remembered what it was like to want to be on my old studio's older competition team, and I wanted to be a good role model for them. I pulled off my sneakers and put my bag in a cubby. I decided to dance in bare feet today. I was wearing a gray cami top and black-and-white leggings. I gave myself a quick spritz with my vanilla scent and inhaled a calming breath.

"Spread out!" Vanessa called out. She turned out the lights and some soft lyrical music rang through the studio.

We all scattered into three rows. I spotted Lily across the room, but she didn't see me. The Bunheads were front and center. Since we were partway through the summer session, I was joining a class in progress. I found a spot on the floor in the back. In my old studio, I'd try to be up front for most classes, but I wanted to ease into it here.

Then Lily turned around and spotted me. She quickly wove between people to get to the back and stood next to me.

I followed the student leading the stretches. We stretched side to side, then did some neck rolls. People were talking a little bit during stretches. When Lily's head was turned toward me, she whispered, "Hi! Aren't you excited?"

"Yeah." I nodded and smiled at her. "Thanks for coming back here."

"Oh, look! Wait for it . . . ," Lily said, pointing to the clock on the wall.

"11:11," we both said as the clock turned. I closed my eyes and made a wish. I'm not telling what it was, but let's just say it had to do with friendship.

Vanessa clapped her hands for our attention.

"We'll start with a new lyrical combo," Vanessa said.

"Did you come from ballet?" I asked Lily. She was wearing a black leotard, pink tights rolled up to her ankles, and a tight bun.

"Yes, a private lesson," she said. "My parents said I have to do two ballet privates a week to keep up my training."

"You're lucky," I said. "I can't take any privates yet."

"Ugh, but it's ballet. They don't let me flip upside down in ballet," she groaned. "Hey, did you see *Dance-Off* last night?"

"Yes!" I lit up. My favorite had been safe! "I was so happy my fave didn't get eliminated."

"Me too," Lily said. "But I also like the hip-hop girl. If those two don't make the final three, I seriously will cry."

"My second favorite is the tap dancer," I said. "He's so precise."

We talked about our show for a few more seconds, until a

singer's voice and a slow song flooded the studio. We all focused our attention on Vanessa. She waited so we could listen to the music and prepare the mood.

"Start with a four-count hold," she said. "Then a lunge, swinging your foot through."

Dances are complicated, so they are taught in combinations. The teacher will break down the moves into eight counts, so you remember dances in these chunks, or combos. Then you put the chunks together. For this combo, Vanessa had us start with a lunge, then reach our right hand toward the sky and arch our backs. Then we finished out the eight counts melting down to a ball, bringing it in. Once we'd practiced each eight-count combo individually, Vanessa said we would run through the whole routine.

"Take it from the top." Vanessa counted off and then we went into the moves.

I watched myself in the mirror as I did the combo. I didn't get mine all the way, but I noticed Megan did easily.

"And again!" Vanessa said. "Watch those feet! Five, six, seven, eight."

The two girls in front of me stepped toward each other and accidentally crashed, and everyone laughed as the music stopped.

"Sorry!" The girls laughed again and hugged each other.

After we got that combo, we moved to the second one: a développé into a jeté. Then some more lyrical moves, ending with a needle—a move where you literally try to make a straight line with your body and leg. I pulled my arms straight above my head and tried to get my foot as high as possible, arching my back. Then I held it.

I did my best to focus on myself, but with the Bunheads in front of me, reflecting back in the mirror, I couldn't help but notice them dance. Riley looked like she was having so much fun, working her facials even as we rehearsed it. Trina was fluid and lovely. And Megan's needle was incredible. She had her leg so straight it was like she was in a perfect split, and she was making it look effortless. She had a really flexible range of motion and worked it every time we did the steps.

We all went through the combo from start to finish, and then applauded for ourselves. Lily turned to me and held out her fist and I punched it.

Vanessa turned off the music.

"Next, line up by the mirrors. It's the moment you've been waiting for all month! Our lyrical freestyle competition!"

Freestyle competition? I looked at Lily, and she looked back.

Someone whooped and everyone laughed.

"We will run three groups. Count off by threes, please!" Vanessa called out. Then she looked over at Lily and me. "If you're a new dancer this month, please come to me."

Lily and I stood up. We went over to Vanessa and joined an older girl who also must've been new. Vanessa explained to us what was happening.

"Every month, we have a dance-off to show off everyone's new skills. Each group will improv for one minute, and we will vote on the winner of each. You three may sit down and observe."

Cool. I slid down to sit on the floor, and Lily sat down next to me, with the other new girl on her other side.

"So we don't have to dance?" Lily whispered. "Whew. I was stressing!"

I knew what she meant. Dancing and being judged when you're new is nerve-racking. But I also had a moment of envy. I loved to dance—and I loved to perform. Sitting on the sidelines was easier, but also, I wondered how I would do if I were up there too.

"Group one out on the floor!" Vanessa called out. "Groups two and three take a seat along the mirror!"

A slow song came on, and group one began to dance.

I watched them all. Some were dancing softly, and some were fierce even in the lyrical style. I sat back and enjoyed watching everyone's unique styles. I thought about what I would do if I went up there. I pictured myself doing a bunch of turns, bringing up my hands dramatically, then reaching toward the audience and sliding into a split on the floor and rolling my head and Vanessa announcing the winner was . . . me! And everyone clapping for me!

Then I flashed back to reality and saw myself in the mirror, sitting on the floor in the corner, twirling the ends of my hair.

"Five . . . four . . . three," Vanessa counted down so everyone could finish up with a strong ending. "Two . . . one. Stop!"

Everyone stopped dancing. The dancers then lined up and turned around the opposite way so they couldn't see us. Vanessa told the seated dancers to raise their hands to secretly vote for their winner.

She pointed at the first girl, and a few dancers quietly raised their hands to vote for her. Vanessa didn't look to us new girls to vote. An older girl won. I could agree with that decision. She had a really good connection to the song, and you could feel she was dancing her emotions. That was something I sometimes had to remind myself about.

"Group two!" Vanessa called out. The next group included

Megan and Trina. The music began, and the girls started dancing. Megan's dancing immediately caught my eye, and when I looked down the line of us at the mirror, I could see a lot of people also watching Megan dance. Trina was really good too, especially her facials as she did elaborate moves one after the other. But when Megan held her leg turn and then stopped and let go of her leg and held it, all eyes were on her.

This time it was practically unanimous.

"The winner of the second group is . . . Megan!" Vanessa announced.

"Group three!" Vanessa called out. Riley and a few other dancers went up to the floor.

"New students!"

Lily elbowed me. Vanessa was looking at us.

"Does she mean us?" she whispered.

"Yes, I do!" Vanessa heard her and replied. "Now that you have observed the process, please join group three."

Lily and I and the other new girl looked at each other like, *Yikes!* I had misread that situation. We *did* have to dance.

Eek!

I followed Lily out onto the dance floor and tried to psych

myself up to compete. There weren't enough girls to hide behind, so everyone was pretty much front and center.

The music came on. So I danced. I just went with the music and danced the moves I'd visualized before. I committed to it, just as I had in my daydream. There was room on the floor, so I did a jeté in second, oversplitting and leaping high in the air. Then I did a turn series that felt right, bringing my hands up dramatically.

"Five . . . four . . . three," Vanessa counted down.

Then I reached toward the audience and slid into a split on the floor, and rolled my head down.

"Two . . . one!"

Everyone stopped dancing. I snapped out of my dance zone to see the class lined up on the floor along the mirror, watching us.

I suddenly felt self-conscious as I turned to face away from the class so I couldn't see the voting.

"To vote for your winner, quietly raise your hand," Vanessa instructed. Just as she had with the previous two groups, I knew she was pointing at each of us for votes.

"Turn around," she told us. "And the winner of group three is . . .

"HARPER. Congratulations, Harper."

Harper? Harper as in me?

Everyone started clapping. I immediately looked apologetically to Lily—but she was clapping harder than everyone. *Eee! Yay!*

I won! I showed DanceStarz I could dance! Woo hoo! I was really excited. I went back to the mirror to sit down with the rest of group three and enjoy my victory.

"I need the three winners back up here, please," Vanessa said.

Top three, baby! I jumped up and stood with my fellow winners on either side, smiling appreciatively.

"Next," Vanessa said, "the finalists will dance off to be the July lyrical freestyle champion."

Oh great, it wasn't just to show off the top three. I had to dance again! *Deep breath, Harper, deep breath.* I didn't have anything planned, so I was just going to have to let the dance flow. I looked at the girl next to me and we smiled at each other. Then I looked at Megan and smiled. She gave me a stone-cold look.

"It's a battle to the death," someone murmured, and people giggled.

"You have one minute to dance," Vanessa said, and turned the music on.

So I danced. I listened to the music for a moment, closed my eyes and raised my arms, and then I went all in.

I started out with a layout and a more simple footwork sequence. I threw everything I had on the floor. I had my toes pointed, my arms in the right position, and I was feeling it, so I went into some pirouettes for a turn series.

"Five . . . four . . . three." Vanessa was giving us the heads-up.

And that's when it happened. Megan did a forward roll right in front of me as if she didn't see me there. *Ack!* I heard everyone gasp. I almost tripped over her, but at the last minute I raised my leg over her and did a side kick over Megan's head.

Whew! Avoided a collision!

I thought Megan would roll out from under me, and I started to lower my leg—but then I realized she was still there! She had started to stand up, apparently thinking I was done dancing.

I didn't have time to really think about it. I pulled my leg up again and I spun around—and my leg went over her head again. Just barely. A few inches down and I would have smacked her in the face with my leg. I heard people gasp.

"Two . . . one."

Megan rolled away from me. I pulled my leg up one last

time and held the pose. *Whew. Done.* That was close. I did not want my first dance-off to be known as the one where I'd kicked the best dancer in the face, thank you. I inhaled deeply, trying to catch my breath.

"Time to vote," Vanessa said.

The three of us turned around with our backs to the rest of the class. I was still breathing hard from that near-miss, while everyone voted silently. When we turned around, I noticed most of the people were looking right at me.

"Our winner is . . . ," Vanessa said, "Harper."

I won.

"Whoooo!" People clapped and pounded the floor. Lily was stamping her feet as well.

I smiled, embarrassed but excited! Okay, this was really cool. Really cool. My first victory at DanceStarz! I got to show my new studio what I was capable of. I looked over at Vanessa, who was smiling at me approvingly. *Yay!*

The only thing that would kill my mood would be to look at Megan, so I said to myself, *Don't look at Megan, don't look at Megan . . .* I peeked at Megan. She wasn't giving anything away with her smile, but I saw her eyes narrow when she caught my glance. *Ouch.* You don't want to know the eye conversation she had with me.

"Harper, as the winner, you get to be featured on Dance-Starz social media," Vanessa said.

"I do?" I asked, surprised. Everyone laughed.

Vanessa took my picture and I smiled for the camera.

"Be prepared to see the trophy emoji!" Trina called out and everyone laughed again.

arper!" Lily came bouncing into Studio C. She was wearing her turquoise dance top with black-and-white polka-dot shorts.

I had arrived early, as I always liked to do, and the studio had been empty. I was sitting on the floor doing butterfly stretches.

"Your polka dots are so cute!" I said.

"Thanks, but let's talk about the real story. Hello, did you see how many likes you got on DanceStarz?!"

"Really?" I answered, trying to play it cool. Then I gave up on that. "Okay, I already know. I was kind of obsessed with looking at it."

DanceStarz had posted a picture taken during my freestyle, while I was midleap. It was a cool picture. And the caption under it read: *July's lyrical freestyle winner: Harper*. And yes, there was a trophy emoji next to it as Trina had said.

"I would be too. I was so excited for you!" she said.

"Thanks," I said. "I'm sure you were great too."

"Meh, lyrical freestyle's not my thing. Years of ballet, and I'm still better at just jumping around." Lily waved it off. She ran and did a round-off back handspring. Then she slid over to sit by me and stretched. "That last move you did made everyone gasp!"

"I just won because of luck," I said. "If Megan hadn't slid near me I wouldn't have done it at all."

I wasn't sure if Megan would be so happy to hear that. I had relived that moment in my mind. Part of me thought that Megan hadn't seen me there. But it was just as likely that she had slid in front of me to get the attention for herself. And if that was the case, it hadn't worked.

"That's not luck, that's mad skills," Lily said, and held out her hand for a fist bump.

I bumped her fist, but pulled it back quickly when the door opened. It was the Bunheads.

"Hello!" I said.

"So, Harper. You really came into the freestyle hard yesterday," Megan said, putting her backpack in a cubby.

And hello to you, too. I wasn't sure what she meant by that, exactly. Was that a good thing or a bad thing?

"Wasn't Harper awesome?" Lily said.

"Mm-hmm," Megan answered. Megan and Riley came right over and started stretching with us. Trina sat down by the cubbies to take off her sneakers.

"Megan, you were awesome too," I said genuinely.

"Harper. It's kind of weird, you just busting in here and trying to take over," Riley said. "By running over Megan. Everyone saw that."

"What? I was just dancing," I said. "If I hadn't leapt, I would have run *into* Megan."

"Mm-hmm," Megan said. "Still, there's some things newbies just should know on their own. Like how to stay in your lane."

"What is that supposed to mean?" Lily challenged.

"Just that she should dance where she's supposed to," Megan said innocently.

"I think we all did great," I said. I'd danced with divas all my life. I didn't want to make waves as the new girl, but I knew I couldn't let her entirely push me around. "But also? I'm proud of myself that I won."

Megan wasn't expecting that. Her eyes narrowed.

"No offense, but I think your win was a fluke," she said. "Enjoy it while it lasts."

The door opened.

"Here's our team! DanceStarz Squad, together as one!" Vanessa walked in.

Yeah . . . no.

We jumped up and plastered happy smiles on our faces.

"Now, let's get right to work. We'll start working on our first group dance today," Vanessa said.

That perked everyone up. What was our first dance as a team going to be? I had an eye conversation with Lily to say I was dying of suspense. Would it be a jazz number? Musical theater? Lyrical?

"Our first piece will be a contemporary dance."

Vanessa had chosen contemporary. Contemporary dances could really range: fast and upbeat, slower and more controlled. I was excited to see what it would be.

"This dance will be called 'Awaken.' The theme will be about discovering new things, new choices, and figuring out a new energy—which feels perfect for this group."

Riley waved her hand wildly.

"What will our costumes be?"

"I'm still deciding," Vanessa said.

She had us start in pyramid formation, and then we went right into the first block of choreography.

Megan was being set up as the featured dancer in the group. It made sense. I knew from lyrical class that Megan was a star in the studio. Megan's tricks and confidence helped keep the attention on her while she was dancing. Vanessa knew what she could count on her for. I hoped someday she'd have that confidence in me. I felt like I had made a little bit of an impression on her by winning the dance-off, and I wanted to keep that momentum going.

"I want this dance to be fun and energetic," Vanessa said. "We want to capture the audience from the first moment."

We learned the next combination.

"High energy!" Vanessa called out. "There will be some intricate movements, and every movement will matter in order for it to work—and for you all to be safe."

This dance had some challenging footwork. I had my toes pointed, my feet turned out, but by the time I was in position, I was a beat behind.

"No, no!" Vanessa called out, shaking her head. She came and stood in front of me and demonstrated. Vanessa did three quick steps.

I copied those three quick steps.

"Yes, like that," Vanessa nodded. "Now get that in sync with everyone else."

What was my issue? The other girls were getting it, even Lily. This combination seemed to move so quickly. By the time I got my arms and feet in position, it seemed the other girls had moved to the leap. They were leaping, and I was following them.

"Harper, you have to explode out of the position quickly," Vanessa said, frustrated. "Megan, show Harper the pacing, please."

Megan stood in front of me and showed me.

"Watch Megan's transition," Vanessa instructed.

I could feel the other girls' eyes on me.

"It's easy," Megan said brightly. "See?"

She did the footwork perfectly.

"Just do that," Megan challenged me. She shot me a fake smile while I tried it. I fumbled.

"Harper, are you feeling comfortable?" Vanessa asked.

"Yes!" I quickly said. "Well—it's just . . . the transition . . . something . . ."

I felt tears spring to my eyes, and I sucked in my breath trying to calm down.

"Maybe her old studio didn't dance hard and she's tired," Megan suggested, giving me an innocent look.

"I dance hard!" I protested.

"Megan, that's not necessary," Vanessa said. "But I do agree, it can be a big adjustment to get used to a new studio."

"Lily got the steps," Megan fake-whispered.

I winced.

"We're going to keep on until it's right," Vanessa said.

And we did. And I couldn't get it right. What was going on with me?!

"I can't believe we have to keep doing this just because *she* can't get it," Megan whispered.

"Wasting everyone's time," Riley agreed.

La, la, la. I tried to block them out and just ignore them.

It was hard.

After class was over, I got up and went straight for my dance bag. Once again, it wasn't where I'd put it. After last class, I had put it into one of the higher cubbies. Now it was in a low cubby. I reminded myself to ask where I was supposed to store my things. I didn't want to be paranoid or suspicious, but . . . I was getting frustrated. I just wanted to go home and be alone for a while.

"Harper." Lily came up to me. "I wanted to see if you could come over to my house."

"To be honest, I'm kind of not feeling great." I felt a lump in my throat, and I swallowed hard. I didn't want to admit how much my fail in class was bothering me.

"But today I get to go home," Lily said. "Most days, I'm going to be stuck waiting for the store to close. But my mother has to go home to wait for a plumber or something. Yay, I get to hang out at home. Boo, I have to spend it by myself unless you come with me?"

Lily gave me a winning smile and posed. I had to smile back at that. I did want to get to know Lily. But I also wanted to go home and just feel sorry for myself for a little bit.

"We could go swimming," Lily kept going. "I have a poooool. You can borrow a bathing suit. We can float away your worries."

"That does sound pretty good." I wavered.

"I'm going to walk on my hands until you say yes," Lily said. She did a handstand and started hand-walking in circles.

"I'm getting tired!" she continued, upside down. "I'm getting dizzy. Say yes, Harper!"

Swimming > sulking.

Lily > loneliness.

"Fine, I don't want to torture you. I'll ask my mom," I said. She landed with a *thunk* on the ground, and we were both smiling.

9

On the drive to Lily's house, her mom asked the usual mom questions: How did I like it here (pretty good so far), what was my favorite subject in school (math), and where would I be going (to the same school as Lily, yay!). She also asked me what yogurt flavors I'd like to see in the store, which was fun. I suggested s'mores and then thought up macarons, which were my favorite dessert to get when I went into New York City.

"I've never had a macaron," Lily said.

"Macarons are amazing. Lemon, pistachio, chocolate . . ." I sighed. "We'll have to find some here."

The plumber was pulling up to Lily's house when we got there, so her mom said we should go straight back to the pool.

Lily's pool was curvy-shaped with a diving board at the deep end. She had white lounge chairs set up along the side.

"You're so lucky you have a pool," I told her. "The best part of living in Florida is swimming."

"Totally. I can't believe I have a pool. And cute new bathing suits. Pick any of them and I'll get towels. There's a little changing room in there." Lily pointed to a large white shed.

I went inside the shed, which was set up with two benches. Three bathing suits and some towels were on one of the benches. I chose an emerald-green top and navy bottoms and put them on.

"Go ahead and get in!" Lily's mom called from the screen porch overlooking the pool. "I'm watching you girls."

I waved to Lily's mother, who waved back.

I went to the shallow end of the pool and sat at the edge, dangling my feet in, letting myself get used to the temperature. The water was pretty warm, so I slid in up to my waist, then held my breath and went underwater. I popped up and then floated on my back. *Ah*. I stared at the bright blue Florida sky, the sun blazing warm on my face. Lily was right. This was a good way to relax and not worry about dance class today. To not worry about how I couldn't get the choreography down and I'd been a beat behind the other girls. And how the Bunheads seemed to think Lily and I had replaced their friends, and obviously I was a poor substitute and—

SPLASH!

Lily jumped in right near my head and sprayed me with water.

"Sorry, not sorry!" She laughed when I sputtered. "You're supposed to be relaxing and not thinking about dance. You don't look relaxed at all."

"I know, I know," I said. "I always think about dance. Usually, it's fun, though."

"Okay, let's dance, then," Lily said. "Let's do the fun part: tumbling!"

"You really like your tumbling, don't you?" I laughed.

"I did gymnastics for four years, but my mom wanted me to switch to ballet," Lily said. "So hopefully this team will be a good combination of those."

Lily threw herself into a back handspring and popped up with her hands straight in the air.

She disappeared underwater and then her legs and feet popped up into a handstand. She held the handstand underwater for a long time, but was wobbling, before she popped back up and took a breath.

"How do you hold your breath like that?" I asked. "Impressive."

"Your turn," Lily said.

I took a deep breath and dove underwater. I felt around for the bottom and put my hands flat on the pool floor. I pushed my feet up and out. I pointed my toes and stayed there for a few seconds before I lost my balance. Then I pushed off and arched my back to resurface.

"Nice and straight," Lily said approvingly.

"Were my toes pointed? Was I wobbling at the end?"

"Your toes were totally pointed. But, okay, you wobbled."

"Like I messed up the steps today." I groaned.

"Hello? You did, like, a hundred pirouettes and a leg hold into a relevé the other day," Lily said. "If I did that, I wouldn't just wobble, I'd fall over on my face."

We both laughed.

"I just wanted to be, you know, perfect." I sighed.

"Well, you weren't," Lily said so matter-of-factly it made me laugh. "And you get a seven-point-five on your handstand."

"I can do better," I promised. "Next round."

"Now the pressure's on me," Lily said. She went under for another handstand. She was super straight and balanced. She stayed under for a long time. A long, long time. Finally, she popped up.

"Wow, you really can hold your breath forever," I said. "Extra points for stamina. Eight out of ten. Extra point off because your toes weren't pointed."

"I always forget the toes." Lily shook her head, smiling. "Back handspring next!" Lily said. She flung herself backward and her feet appeared, and then her head again.

"That was so fast!" I was impressed. "You're so good at tumbling. Nine!"

I flung myself into a back handspring. Lily graded me an 8. Then we each did a front flip with our legs tucked in (Harper 8, Lily 8.5), and a back walkover (Harper 8, Lily 7.5).

"What do I need to work on?" I asked. "Seriously."

"I guess your speed," Lily said. "Some of the moves require power. And holding your breath longer."

"You're great at those," I said.

"I need to work on my legs and feet," Lily said. "That's what my ballet teachers always told me. It's so hard to focus on every little thing, you know?"

Oh, I knew.

Lily pulled herself out of the pool and ran around to the diving board. She stood at the end and held her hand up high like a gymnast before a vault. She ran to the end of the diving board and . . .

"CANNONBALL!" Lily yelled. She plunged into the water with a big splash, spraying water all over me.

"Okay, I was *not* expecting that." I laughed when she emerged.

"Ten out of ten, right?" Lily asked.

"Well, your arms were a little crooked wrapped around your knees . . . ," I teased.

"Picky, picky," Lily said. Then she splashed water at me. Water fight!

"Girls!" Lily's mother came outside.

"Oh, I'm sorry," I apologized, sputtering from the water.

"There's nothing to be sorry about," Lily's mother said. "Water is for fun. I'm bringing something I thought you might enjoy."

She held up two items that shimmered in the sun. They were actual mermaid tails! One was an aquamarine-green mix and the other was a purple-blue mix.

"They're waterproof. Go ahead and put them on to swim," said Lily's mom.

"Mom, these are so cool! Thank you!" Lily jumped out of the pool.

"You've been really helpful at the store, so I wanted to bring you a present," Lily's mother said. She smiled at our thanks.

"These are so cute," I told her. I swam to the edge of the pool, and Lily's mother handed me the shimmery purple-and-blue tail. I sat on the pool steps and pulled it on. "Great timing that I was here when they came in."

"Actually, I'm guessing they came before but my mom hid them until I had a friend over," Lily said. "Remember? No friends, loser."

"We just moved here!" I said. "I have no friends here either. We're both losers together. Loser mermaids!"

I flipped up my tail, and the flippers at the end sprayed water everywhere. It took me a second to figure out how to move as I swam across the shallow end. Lily followed behind me, and we both wiggled our tails to move out to the deep end. We ducked underwater and pushed off from the side of the pool. I mermaid swam, with Lily right by my side.

Ahh. I was relaxed. And it got even better, because Lily's mother brought out a snack tray.

"Sugar Plums just got new toppings in," her mom said. "Maybe you can taste-test them."

"Thank you!" Lily and I swam-raced to the tray.

There was a bowl of mini pretzel twists and a bowl of sour gummy kids. And Lily's mom had given us some lemonade with raspberries. We were quiet for a minute while we both drank and snacked.

"I love all of these toppings." I broke the silence as I fished a raspberry out of my glass and popped it in my mouth. "This day got much better. Thanks for having me over."

"Thanks for coming over," Lily said quietly. "I'm so bored with no friends here. And I look at my friends' posts and I feel so homesick. The girls are starting lacrosse practices now, and I miss the team and my old dance team too."

"Me too," I said. "I miss my friends, my team, and my house. It's so weird to wake up and be living a completely different life. It's like, hello, who am I now? But wait—you play lacrosse?"

"Played, past tense," she said. "My parents want me to focus, and that was the deal when I asked to do competition dance instead of ballet. They want to make sure I have enough time for ballet. Do you play sports?"

"I did soccer for like a day," I said. "But I wanted to be on the dance team more. And I loved my old studio. My dad wasn't even looking for a new job, and suddenly he just came home and said, *Let's have an adventure! Let's move our whole lives!*"

"Same." Lily nodded. "My parents were like, *We bought a new store*, and suddenly I was just dumped here."

We both drank our lemonade silently, leaning on the edge of the pool with our elbows, mermaid tails swishing in the water.

"I guess there are worse places to be dumped," I said and popped a gummy in my mouth.

"Definitely. But I'm glad someone else gets it," Lily said.

Me too.

s everybody stretched?" Vanessa called out. "Let's rehearse what we've learned. Then we'll add the second block to your routine."

After swimming at Lily's last night, we had rehearsed the dance steps over and over in her room. I hoped it was enough. I took my place off to the left side of the pyramid with Trina and Megan.

Vanessa counted the beats: "One, TWO, three, four . . . ball change and—"

I was on it! I had it . . . five, six, seven, eight . . . Lily shot me a little smile. I got my posture, my arms in position, my feet . . .

And I lost it.

"Break!" Vanessa called out. "Let's try that last combo again. Keep your stance wide, but you have to move quicker to stay on beat."

Vanessa didn't call me out, but I could sense everyone looking over again. I closed my eyes and pictured the steps in my head.

"And . . ." Vanessa counted off again.

Nope. I stumbled again.

"Harper!" Megan blew out her breath, frustrated. "Can't you speed that up?"

"I'm trying," I said. I was. I was *really* trying.

What was my issue? I was used to picking up choreography. I was realizing the footwork in this routine was much faster than what I was used to with my old studio—but apparently not faster than the Bunheads and Lily were used to. Lily was so athletic. I could see her moving fast. My strengths were slow, lovely movements. Obviously, I'd danced fast before, but this group was faster than fast.

I needed to pick up the pace.

"Let's move ahead and learn part two," Vanessa said. "Then we'll practice them together."

The second half of the routine started out better for me. We had more of a lyrical focus, so I didn't mess this one up. My arms flowed, making different shapes.

"Nice, Harper!" Vanessa called out. "Everyone see how Harper's movements match the music? Look at her arms."

Yesss. Lily gave me a thumbs-up. I twirled and I leapt, feeling much better. I was completely in sync with the rest of the team.

"Riley, turn your left foot out," Vanessa said. "Trina, dramatic hands. Lily, be more fluid. Hm, this section needs more life to it."

"Vanessa!" Megan said. "How about we do the turns into the big stag leap, aka the move that the judges loved when we did it at junior nationals?"

Megan turned to me.

"Our group came in first," she informed me.

"That was a crowd-pleaser," Vanessa said. "I'm willing to give that a try. We can move directly into that after the first combination."

Ergh. I groaned inwardly. This sounded like what I was struggling with before. My jumps were okay, but not so quick after an intense combination.

Megan went up to demonstrate the move. The Bunheads, who had done it before, copied her flawlessly.

"Break it down slower for Lily and Harper," Vanessa instructed. "This is new to them."

Five . . . six . . . seven . . . eight . . .

I got the first part down, but when we sped up, disaster struck. *Crash!*

I leapt smack into Riley. Riley stumbled into Megan, who went off balance.

"Ow!" Megan yelped. "What the heck?"

"Sorry, sorry," I apologized. "The half turn right before is killing me!"

"Perhaps we should wait on this section," Vanessa said.

"But it's our signature move!" Megan shot me a look. I wasn't going to mess with that.

"It's fine! I'll pick it up."

But I didn't. We ran through it two more times, and while I didn't knock anyone over, I didn't get it right, either. I was feeling seriously frustrated by the time we went to cool down.

I went over to the cubbies quickly, already knowing my dance bag would have been moved to a different spot. I was used to it by now.

"Harper," Lily came up to me. "Your other pirouettes and turns were really great. Weren't you so happy when Vanessa told you that? I didn't get anything called out today. I think I'm blending in too much."

"I'd rather blend in than stand out the way I'm standing

out right now," I told her miserably. "Can you help me with the setup into that leap? You did that immediately."

Lily demonstrated it for me. Then I tried. But I wasn't getting it.

"Sorry," I said. "I can't get it right."

"I don't know, your technique is so good, it's . . . I'm not sure. You have to loosen up and be fast, I guess?"

"That's my problem, I can't be loose," I said. "Or fast enough."

"I'm a terrible teacher, sorry," Lily said.

I don't think anyone is going to be able to teach me, I thought miserably.

Some younger boys and girls started filing in for a jazz class, so we got our stuff to leave.

"I have to go over to Sugar Plums," Lily said. "Want to come?"

"Let me ask," I told her, trying to sound less miserable. I was really happy Lily was on my team. But I was feeling like such a downer. I didn't want her inviting me because she had nobody better to ask. Or worse, because she felt sorry for me. I needed to pick it up.

When we went out the door, the Bunheads were standing together talking. I almost tried to sneak past them, but then pulled it together. This was my team. I couldn't hide from them.

Plus, maybe if they got to know me better, I could get in sync with them. Or, if nothing else, they'd stop hiding my bag.

"We should invite them," I whispered to Lily. "Team bonding."

"Bunheads!" Lily called out. "Do you want to get fro-yo?"

"Can't," Megan said, at the same time Trina and Riley said: "I can!"

Riley and Trina looked at Megan.

"My sister can't pick me up until after her play rehearsal, so I'm stuck here," Trina said.

"I'm stuck until Quinn finishes mini ballet." Riley glanced at Megan. "And I'm really hungry."

"Well! Okay!" Lily said. "We have new toppings."

"Sour kids and pretzels," I added, in the know about *something*, at least.

"Oh, Megan loves sour kids," Riley said.

Megan paused, and the other Bunheads waited hopefully.

"Actually, I can." She changed her mind without explanation. "Let's go."

The girls went out to the studio lobby and found the moms. My mom was sitting with Megan's and Riley's mothers.

"How did it go?" Mom asked me.

If she wanted an honest answer to that question, she should never ask it in front of others.

"May I go get fro-yo with the team?" I deflected the question.

"Mom, we're going to that fro-yo place," Megan said to her mom. "I need money."

Megan's mother wordlessly pulled out her bag and handed her a credit card.

"May I?" I asked Mom. She looked over at Hailey, who was sitting on the carpet, playing rock-paper-scissors with Riley's little sister, who was in ballet gear. I was glad at least two members of our families were getting along.

"Well, your sister seems happily occupied," Mom said, reaching for her bag. "Go ahead. We'll come over in a little while. I wouldn't mind a frozen yogurt myself. I'll trade you a yogurt if you'll watch your sister for me later tonight."

"Deal," I said.

As we walked over to Sugar Plums, Megan and the rest of the girls ignored Lily and me as they watched a funny video on Megan's phone. As soon as we got to Sugar Plums, we all grabbed some treats after saying hi to Lily's parents.

"What'd you get?" Trina asked.

"Original tart with sour kids," I said.

"Makes sense since your class performance was sour." Megan nodded. "Let's get to the real problem here. What are we going to do about your dancing, Harper?"

I almost choked on a sour kid candy.

"What *problem*?" Lily asked, furious.

"Harper isn't keeping up with the choreo." Megan shrugged. "And we can't have her messing up the routine for everybody."

I couldn't believe this. I felt my face blaze red, and I looked around to see everyone's reactions. Trina and Riley were looking down at the table and Lily's jaw had dropped.

"Harper and I are new and just learning," Lily said, sticking up for me. "You guys have danced together forever, so obviously, you're going to be in sync faster."

"*You're* doing fine," Megan said. "I was talking about Harper and her weaknesses. I think it needs to be addressed. No offense, Harper."

I almost burst into tears right there. Was I really messing up so badly? Lily reached under the table and squeezed my hand.

"That seems kind of harsh, Megan," Lily said. "Vanessa is our dance teacher, not you."

"You're new, so you don't know this, but . . . ," Riley said. "Megan practically was team captain last year. Not officially or anything. But pretty much."

"No, remember?" Trina shook her head. "Isabelle was team captain last year and Bella was second captain?"

"Well, if the Bells had gotten some sickness, then Megan

pretty much would have been captain," Riley said. "Like if they got the flu. Or chicken pox. Or . . ."

I regained my composure.

"Okay, I get it. Look. I know I'm messing up the dance steps," I said. "I just need to get better."

"That's right," Megan said. "That's what I was saying."

"It's just the *jump*," Lily said.

"TBH, it's also the performance and facials," Megan said.

"I was trained differently." I jumped in to defend myself. "I can learn all of that. It's been one week."

"Let's just skip the tricky steps until we have time to practice more," Lily suggested.

"Do you know what DanceStarz is known for?" Megan said. "Our performance skills and our fancy footwork. We've worked really hard the past couple years, and now is our time to show everyone what we can do. We can't go backward!"

Megan whipped out her phone.

"We need to show Isabelle and Bella that even though they left us for Energii and they think they're all that, we don't need them," Megan said. "Look what they posted."

She set her phone on the table and played a video. Six girls were on the dance floor, lined up in formation. Their arms and legs were perfectly matching each other. Their entire group did a long turn series in perfect sync, flawlessly, to open their routine. Right into the big stag leap.

Now I knew why Megan was so determined to include those moves. She wanted to prove herself to her former teammates—now rivals.

I wanted to prove myself too.

"I get it. I want to be just as good as these girls. I really do." I looked squarely at Megan. "I like to win too."

I thought I saw a glimmer of respect in Megan's eye.

"We know you can win," Trina said. "You won the dance-off! Remember when you leapt over Megan? That was so cool."

Megan's face turned back into a pout. Trina turned to me.

"Why don't you take extra private sessions with Vanessa?" Trina asked.

That actually was a good idea.

"That might help." Megan nodded. "Ask her ASAP."

"I will," I said, taking a bite of my now-melty yogurt. "Now you all don't have to worry about it anymore."

Ta-da! There was the solution. Everything would be better after I'd taken some private lessons.

No private lessons," Mom said firmly.

"But, Mom," I protested, "I *need* private lessons."

I pulled the seat belt and buckled myself into the car. My mom started the car and pulled out of the parking lot of the dance studio.

"Turn on the music!" Hailey called from the backseat.

"One sec. I need to talk to Mom first," I said. "It's important. I *have* to do private sessions with her."

"Did Vanessa say that to you?" Mom asked.

"No—not directly," I said. "But—"

"I'm sorry, but they are not in the budget," Mom said.

"Moving was a big expense, and you know I haven't found a job yet. Private lessons will have to wait."

"But, Mom! You don't understand!" After what just happened at the studio, I needed privates! I knew I was whining, but this was *important*.

"Harper," Mom said sharply. "Do *you* understand that you already are taking dance five times a week? Have you thought about how many times a week your sister is taking any classes in any activities?"

"Two!" Hailey piped up. "Only two classes for the poor, neglected little sister."

Ugh. They were kind of right.

"I'm sorry." I sighed. "And I'm sorry, Hailey. You're right."

"Yay!" Hailey said. "You can make it up to me by playing with me when we get home—anything I want."

"Perfect, because Harper agreed to babysit for you when we get home," Mom said. "Also, please stop playing with your hair."

I dropped my ponytail, but not my attitude. I sank back into the seat. *Ugh*. None of this was going well. Oh, right. One more reason I wished I hadn't gone for yogurt after class. First I was humiliated, now I'm stuck babysitting.

"We can do the 'What's in My Cup?' Challenge!" Hailey said.

For that challenge, we put mystery liquids in each other's cups and had to drink them and guess the ingredients.

"Let's not!" My mom shut that down too. "Do you remember the mess you made last time?"

I did remember. I'd given Hailey a lovely concoction of orange juice, coconut water, and . . . hot sauce. It had been kind of funny when she'd jumped up, knocked over the glass, and spit the drink all over the table.

"But I guessed it right, so I won the challenge!" Hailey raised the roof.

"I'm so proud," Mom said as we pulled into the driveway. "And no, you're not doing that again."

"Then let's do Dance Challenge!" Hailey said.

If I were in the mood, playing Dance Challenge with Hailey was actually pretty fun. I wasn't in the mood. But I wasn't in the mood to argue with my mother, either.

"Okay," I said. "Let's get you into costume."

We went into the house and straight up to my room. I opened my closet door on the side where my old costumes were kept.

"Which one can I wear?" Hailey asked.

"You choose," I said, waving my hand toward the closet.

"Really?" Hailey was excited. "Any of them?"

"Well, not my one from nationals. Or my Dorothy costume. Or Princess Leia. Or the burgundy rhinestone or the white beaded halter top—"

"How about this one?" Hailey pulled a yellow dress out. It was one of my favorites.

"I guess you can wear that one," I agreed.

"Really?" Hailey squealed and went to the bathroom to change. "What are you going to wear?"

"I'll just keep this on." I didn't feel like dealing. My tank and shorts were comfy.

"What? You can't dance-off in boringness!" Hailey protested. "Don't ruin my fun."

I thought about Hailey's response in the car that she didn't get to take dance classes or do anything fun. I guess the least I could do was hang out with her. I shuffled through my old costumes. Not the neon green stretchy one-piece, the pale pink tutu, or the royal-blue tap costume. I pulled out a black long-sleeved leotard with a sheer black skirt and slipped it on. That felt like my mood.

"Ready for makeup!" Hailey called from the bathroom.

After costume, we always did makeup. I had a case full of makeup that I used at competitions. Makeup helped fit the mood of the pieces and the costumes, and helped you get in character. It also highlighted your features onstage under the lights. Hailey wasn't allowed to wear makeup out of the house, so she was excited when I let her use my makeup at home.

Hailey sat on the tall stool in front of the bathroom mirror.

"I want to sparkle," Hailey said.

"Close your eyes," I told her. I swiped some glittery makeup on over her eyelids. Then I pressed on a few tiny silver and fuchsia jewel stickers to her cheeks.

I slicked on a shiny lip gloss. I put her hair up in the style I thought looked cutest on her: two side ponytails.

"Done," I said.

"Can I wear your jewelry?" she asked me hopefully.

I had a bunch of accessories from competitions that coordinated with my dance costumes that Hailey liked to play with too. Pins, earrings, hair clips, combs, ponytail holders, bracelets, bun holders, and chokers. A lot of them had rhinestones, so they sparkled, too.

"Sure, whatever," I said. She pulled out a clip shaped like a giant bow and put it in her hair.

"I'll go pick music," she said.

I did my own makeup quickly. I pulled out a palette with darker colors. Smoky eye and black eyeliner, done shakily and not well. A dark purple lipstick. I looked at myself in the mirror. I had crazy postdance hair, so I pulled a black cap over it and went back out.

"Oh." Hailey frowned. "You look scary."

"You chose your look, I chose mine," I said.

"Dance Challenge rules: Contestants will be scored not on dance skill, but on enthusiasm and overall amazingness."

I nodded.

"First contestant is . . . ," Hailey said. "Hailey!"

As I expected, she picked a peppy new pop song from her favorite singer. I turned off the lights and clicked on the little white blinking strand of lights that looped over my bed. Hailey danced around the room. Hailey actually was a naturally good dancer. My old dance teacher had always tried to get her to join a team because she's flexible, tumbles, and has good stage personality. She twirled, did a back bend, and jumped around, occasionally jumping up onto my ottoman and then leaping off.

I felt antsy. I felt like she was wasting valuable practice time that I needed to work on my footwork. I secretly did the routine on the floor, keeping the top of my body straight so I wouldn't get caught.

Step, step, step, step.

Hailey jumped off the bed and did a closing pose with her arms crossed and a smug look on her face.

"Harper, were you paying attention?" Hailey frowned. "You're looking at your feet."

"Uh." *Busted.* "I'm just stretching them to get ready to dance."

My sister raised an eyebrow.

"You better bring it." Hailey pointed at me. "Challenge!"

Well, this would be an opportunity to practice the steps. I scrolled through her music choices and picked a song.

"Harper? HARPER!" Hailey had to yell over the pounding beat of the music. "This song is kind of intense."

"I know!" I yelled back. I needed intense right now.

I started practicing the dance. I gave up on the arms and just focused on the footwork. Why couldn't I get that one leap-step combination? *Step, step, step . . .*

"Harper?" Hailey said my name hesitantly. "I said Dance Challenge. Not sitting there barely moving."

My real challenge was figuring out the footwork into the turn before the stag leap. *Ugh!* Fine, I'll show her a dance challenge! I felt my emotions bubble up into anger, so I danced it out. I slammed my fists on the bed, I kicked at my chair— oops—knocking it over.

The music suddenly stopped as Hailey hit mute.

"So aggressive," Hailey said. "Are you still mad you can't do private lessons? Are you mad at me?"

"No, no." I didn't want Hailey to think it was her fault. I might as well be honest. "I'm not so mad. I'm mostly stressed. Our first group dance is complicated and really fast. I'm not getting it right."

"Tell Mom," Hailey said.

"I don't want her to worry about it," I said. "I don't want it to be big drama."

"Tell Miss Vanessa," Hailey said.

I didn't want Vanessa to think I couldn't do something even before our first competition. I didn't want her to regret her decision to choose me for the team. But maybe Hailey was right. If I didn't get help . . . I shuddered.

"Oh wait, we have to vote for our challenge winner," Hailey said, and started a drumroll on the bed and then stopped. "Do you want a pity vote to cheer you up?"

"Definitely not," I said. "I never want a pity vote."

"Then let's get down to business," Hailey said in an announcer's voice. "We are down to the final two, but one dancer will be leaving us tonight. Judges, who do you vote for for elimination?"

"Sadly, I vote for Harper," I said.

"I have to vote for Harper as well," Hailey said. "So the dancer who will going home is . . . Harper."

"Thank you for this opportunity," I said, and then fake-broke down into tears. "Boo hoo! Boo hoo!"

"Please put your hands together for our winner, Hailey!" Hailey jumped around. "Let's close the show with a tribute to our losing contestant, loser Harper."

Hailey imitated my mad dancing. She turned the song back on even louder, and stamped on the floor and pounded her fists on the bed in an aggressive dance.

"Actually, this is kind of fun!" she shouted. "Come dance."

I joined her. It was a good emotional release. We raged together. I whirled around, letting it all out. I danced like nobody was watching.

Suddenly, the door pushed open—and Mo came in. Mo looked around at our crazy scene.

"Ahoooo!" Mo began howling with the music.

Then he spun around in circles really fast with me.

Hailey and I started cracking up.

"He's dancing for us!" Hailey said.

"And singing for you," I told her. "Thank you for your support, Mo."

I meant that for Hailey, too.

I didn't get a chance to talk to Vanessa before team rehearsal, because she was teaching back-to-back classes. I tried to come in just a couple minutes before class started so the Bunheads wouldn't get to ask me about the private lessons.

I put my dance bag in a higher cubby, since it had been moved from a lower one last time, and went to sit near Lily, who was doing lunges.

"Hi!" She seemed happy to see me. She tilted her head at the clock on the wall.

"11:11," she whispered to me.

"Make a wish," we both said.

My wish was that I would rock this dance today. Or at least not knock anyone over.

"I have some exciting news," Vanessa said. "Instead of merely walking in the parade, we have been invited to ride on the float sponsored by Sugar Plums frozen yogurt store."

"Whoo!" We cheered. I high-fived Lily. It would be fun to represent her parents' new store, especially instead of walking.

Trina did a pageant wave.

"I think it would be an excellent time to debut our new team to the community," Vanessa said. "So while the rest of the studio is marching on the street . . ."

She paused for dramatic effect.

"DanceStarz Squad will be performing its first public dance on the float!"

Everyone cheered again, including me. But my cheer was definitely more hesitant than everyone else's. I know teams that can pick up choreography in a few hours, and we had two more days. But would two more days solve my timing issues?

I needed to talk to Vanessa about it. Maybe I could suggest that everyone else do the footwork and I just do a pose? But then that might make it looked like I thought I should be the featured dancer, when I was definitely the opposite of that.

"Will we get costumes now?" Riley asked. I was getting the

idea that Riley was really into costumes, and probably fashion. Her dance outfits were always on point. Today, she was wearing a white racerback dance top with a hot pink stripe and matching leggings.

"Yes," Vanessa said, and everyone cheered. "They will have a theme to reflect the Sugar Plums float. I'll tell you more about that after we practice the routine."

"I hope they're cute!" Lily whispered to me.

Me too! And include magical abilities to make its wearer in sync with her team?

Vanessa wasn't done.

"For now, we're going to tweak the team dance a bit. Since it's going to be on a float, we need to adapt for the space."

Did this mean what I thought it did? Half of me hoped she was cutting out the moves that were messing me up, because that would be a relief. But if she did, that would put a target on me.

"So that being said, we are cutting that tricky sequence," Vanessa confirmed.

Everyone turned to look at me. Megan's eyes narrowed. Yup, the target was on me. *Ouch.*

"Let's run through the dance now without that combination," Vanessa said. "We'll substitute an easier jump sequence."

"It's okay, Harper," Lily whispered to me.

We ran through the routine.

I had to admit it was so much easier for me without the leaps and jumps combo. The rest of rehearsal went smoothly.

I felt the momentum of the dance moving me as I turned in perfect sync with the other four girls, and then we closed. Megan was in the middle, with her arm in the air. Riley and Trina were on either side, their arms outstretched. Lily and I were on the ground in front of them, each doing splits.

I felt energized. And happy.

"Whoo!" Lily shouted, and she and I gave each other double high fives. This excitement and support was what I'd wanted when I'd joined the dance team. It felt good.

After we finished, we went back to change into our street clothes and gathered into a group.

"Nice job, team," Vanessa said. "Now, about your costumes. With such short notice, we're going to stay simple. Since we're representing Sugar Plums, your costume theme will be—"

"Plums!" Trina happily shouted.

"No, not plums." Vanessa smiled and shook her head.

"Plums? What would we wear?" Megan turned to Trina. "Giant round purple costumes?"

"Sure!" Trina wasn't swayed.

"You'll each wear the color of a frozen yogurt flavor," Vanessa said. She brought a box into the room. We opened it up to find pastel costume dresses. They were so pretty: a lace leotard on top and flowy chiffon cascade skirt.

"Megan, you'll be original flavor because you are our original member of the studio." Vanessa gave her a white costume.

"First and fabulous!" Megan held it up to herself and posed happily.

"Riley, you'll be strawberry." Vanessa gave Riley a pink dress.

"Because I'm the second member of the studio?" Riley asked. "I don't get it."

"It's because you said your favorite color is pink," Vanessa said. "Lily, you'll be blueberry. Or I suppose it could be cotton candy." Vanessa gave her a baby blue dress. I was happy for her that she'd gotten something close to her favorite color for her first dance.

"Cotton candy works." Lily grinned. She took her dress happily.

"Trina, you'll be lemon." She gave her a pale yellow dress. "And, Harper, you'll be mint chocolate chip."

I took my mint green dress, pleased. It was really pretty.

"I love them," Megan said definitively. "We're going to look incredible on the float."

"We also have an opportunity to make the float itself look incredible by helping to decorate it," Vanessa said. "Follow me to the back room."

We followed her to the back of the studio, to a space that looked like a giant storage room. On the floor were huge wooden cutouts in the shapes of ice-cream cones, painted in the same colors of our costumes.

"Frozen yogurt cones!" Lily said happily. "My dad had them made to attach to the sides of the float."

Vanessa was wheeling a large three-tiered table toward us.

"The arts cart!" Riley was practically jumping up and down.

"You can embellish the cardboard decorations to create chocolate chips, sprinkles, and other toppings," Vanessa said. "And you can do the same on your costumes if you want. Have at it."

We all went over to the table. There were containers of gemstones, beads, pompoms, and rhinestones, sparkling in so many colors.

"Wow," I said. "I love crafts."

"Isn't this cool?" Riley said, genuinely smiling at me. "Vanessa lets us embellish our stuff here sometimes. Our jackets, our spirit sticks, our props . . ."

"Riley embellishes *everything*," Megan said, rolling her eyes.

"My phone case! My dance duffel! My team jacket!" Riley had no shame.

"She gets it, already," Megan snapped. "Stop talking, start embellishing."

"Yay!" Riley started to dig through the tubs. We all got started.

"My mint chocolate chip needs some chocolate chips," I said. I collected my supplies and brought them over to the floor next to the green wooden fro-yo cone. I used black rhinestones to represent chocolate chips. I thought it would look classic against the mint green color. I used tweezers to pluck out the ones I wanted. I decided to scatter mine around, just like chocolate chips would be. I dotted glue around randomly.

Trina and Lily were using different colors for rainbow sprinkles on theirs. Trina was scattering hers, like I was doing.

"Rainbow sprinkles, like my favorite color," Trina was saying happily.

"Rainbow is not a color," Megan said.

"Rainbow is my favorite," Trina insisted. "Rainbows have red, which is strong; orange, which I love because it's pretty much nobody's favorite color, poor orange; cheerful yellow; green—"

"Okay! Okay!" Megan groaned. "We get it."

"See?" Trina smiled happily and went back to her gluing.

Lily was lining her rhinestones just along the border of her costume.

"Rhinestoning makes me crazy," she said to me, stretching her arms over her head. "I have no patience for this."

I actually liked rhinestoning. It felt like I was doing an art project. It was a challenge to do it as perfectly as I wanted to: The glue would gloop out too much or smear; the rhinestone would stick to my finger or the wrong spot. But it was also relaxing, and I loved the sparkly finished product.

"Do you want my help?" I offered.

"Thanks, but I think I'll go for the minimalist look," Lily said, pressing her last rhinestone. "Meaning, finishing as soon as possible . . . and done!"

She jumped up and went to do handstands against a wall.

I tentatively slid my outfit closer to the Bunheads. I looked at their costumes.

Megan was using iridescent gems that shimmered in different soft colors when they light hit them.

"Megan, that's pretty," I told her.

"I know, right?" Megan said, covering her top so that it was almost all rhinestones with the fabric peeking through. "I'm so good at this. You should see the one I did with my mom for the costume I wore when I won regionals for a jazz/funk dance."

"I love costuming," Riley said happily. Riley was bedazzling her dress in an elaborate geometric pattern.

"Wow, that's cool," I told her. "You like fashion, right?"

Riley was always dressed stylishly in a laid-back way. Right now, she was wearing a black-and-white-plaid shirtdress, a choker, and white sneakers.

"Thanks. I think I might want to be a fashion designer with my own clothing line," Riley said. "And also a Rockette and a football cheerleader."

I also thought it would be cool to have a clothing line. Today, I had on a white varsity tee and slightly baggy boyfriend jeans. Chill and comfortable but really cute.

"I'm going to be a dancer on Broadway, and a supermodel," Megan said. She was wearing a cute outfit too: a cropped tee and high-waisted skinny jeans with a tear in the knee.

"If I can't dance, I'll be a choreographer," Trina said. "Or maybe a teacher. And a mom."

"What do you want to be, Lily?" I called over to her as I dotted some glue.

"Ugh, I don't know," Lily said.

"A dancer?" Trina asked her.

"I don't knoooow," Lily said. "What do you want to be, Harper?"

"Maybe a dancer on Broadway. Or a backup dancer for a celebrity," I said hesitantly. "Or something with makeup, like doing makeup tutorials."

Doing makeup was kind of like doing artwork, both of which I loved.

"You like doing makeup?" Lily asked me. "I hate doing mine. Maybe you can help me for competitions."

"Sure," I said. "I also love doing hair. I do my sister's hair and I always did my dolls' hair."

"Oh, my mom is going to be so happy," Lily said. "She can't stand doing my makeup and hair."

"I love makeup too!" Megan said. "I totally want to have my own kits and makeup channel. My line is going to be called Megan's Makeup. . . ."

Megan took over the conversation, telling us the different colors of her makeup line. The rest of us quietly worked on our costumes.

I finished the last of my "chips" on my leotard, pleased with the results. I looked around at everyone's outfits.

"We are going to look amazing," I announced.

"Our costumes, at least," Megan sniffed. "Too bad, since

our dance could look more amazing. It's so basic now."

"Without the tricky steps and jumps?" Riley asked, and Megan nodded.

My cheeks flamed red.

"We're going to be on a float," Lily pointed out. "It's not a competition."

"Yeah," Megan sighed loudly. "At least it's only a parade for our town. It's not like Energii will be there."

"hy is Energii here?" Megan hissed.

"You have *got* to be kidding me." Riley looked worried.

Uh-oh.

It was parade day! We were in the parade parking lot meeting spot, doing last-minute adjustments to our buns and our pastel costumes, when a white van decorated with bright orange and yellow starbursts pulled up next to us. A team of girls in white leotards with metallic glitter patterns in silver, bronze, and black on them filed out of the van.

"Isabelle! Bella!" Trina excitedly called out and waved.

Trina ran over to two of the girls and grabbed their hands. They reluctantly let her pull them toward us.

"Look who's here!" Trina said.

The Bells.

"Hi!" The Bunheads went to hug the two girls from the other team. The response didn't seem too enthusiastic.

"We didn't know you were going to be here," Riley said. "Energii isn't even from this town."

"You haven't returned any of our texts," Trina added.

"Yeah, we've been super busy," the smaller girl with the black hair in braids wearing a white-and-bronze leotard responded. "New studio, new team, you know."

"I do know! I'm new here," Lily stepped in. "I'm Lily. You must be Isabelle and Bella. I've seen your team videos. You're really good."

"Bella and I have SO many new followers since we joined Energii." The taller girl with light blond hair wearing a white-and-silver leo shrugged.

"But, wait, why is Energii even here?" Megan asked. "Like Riley said, the studio isn't even in this town."

"One of the dancer's dads is a dentist here, so we're dancing on his float," Bella said.

"Oh!" It hit me. I pointed at Isabelle's white-and-silver leotard. "Are you supposed to be teeth with braces on them?"

"I'm a filling. You know, for a cavity," Isabelle said.

"You're a dancing cavity?" Megan asked.

"I'm a *filling*," Isabelle said. "The people with black are the cavities. Bella is gum disease."

"Gingivitis!" Bella corrected her, pointing at her bronze stripes. "They said I'm gingivitis. Not gum disease, ew."

I tried not to laugh, but I let out a snort.

"Uh, who are you?" Isabelle whipped her head toward me.

"I'm Harper." I regained my composure. "I just moved here too."

"Mm-hmm," Isabelle said. "What are you guys supposed to be?"

"We're representing a new frozen yogurt place," Lily said. "Sugar Plums. Check it out!"

"I'm lemon fro-yo with rainbow sprinkles," Trina said. "Hey, Bells, remember when we did the routine where we were in a rainbow? ROYGBIV?"

"Oh, yeah." Isabelle softened for a second. "We won platinum."

"That's when I did my side aerial, but, Megan, you didn't

have yours down yet," Bella said. "So Trina's lemon, Riley's berry something, and what's Megan?"

"Megan is obviously vanilla, because she's boring." Isabelle cracked herself up.

"I'm original tart!" Megan said.

"Even better!" Isabelle laughed. "Original tart for a sour-puss."

Megan's face dropped. I felt sorry for her.

"She's original because she's the original member of the studio," Trina said. "Remember when we all started at Dance-Starz? It's so weird we're not on the same team with you any-more, Bells."

"And now you're the competition." Megan had regained her composure.

"Oh, you're not *our* competition," Isabelle said.

"Right, because this is noncompetitive! It's only a parade," I said, still trying to diffuse the tension.

"No, I meant because Energii will blow your studio away." Isabelle copped an attitude. "You're new, so maybe you don't know you are *not* in our league. There's no competition."

She and Bella fist-bumped.

"Hmph," Megan sniffed. "Not sure how you can be so

confident when you don't even know what we're bringing. Our secret weapons."

Megan pointed to Lily and me.

Wait, what? Secret weapons? Lily and I looked at each other like, *What?!*

"Bring it," Isabelle said. "You're our rivals now."

"And you're traitors," Bella said. "You chose to stay on DanceStarz even though—"

"Bella!" Isabelle interrupted her. "We have to go. But we'll be watching, DanceStarz. Very. Closely."

That sounded like a threat.

"Why did she say *we're* traitors?" Riley asked.

"I don't even know." Megan frowned. I could tell she was upset.

"Are we still friends with them?" Trina asked.

I was guessing the answer to that was no. The Bunheads stood there, all frowning.

"Well! That was fun!" Lily said sarcastically.

"Yeah—no," Megan said. "All right, you heard what just happened. We need to show these bad teeth what we can do. We need to outdance them and outshine them. The Bells are going to be sorry."

Suddenly, this not-a-competition was feeling really competitive. Megan started walking quickly, and I hurried to keep up as we tried to find our float. We wove in between a scouting troop, a float for a Moose Lodge with a giant moose on it, and a fire truck. Then we passed a marching band, and you couldn't miss it:

It was a giant papier-mâché frozen yogurt cup with a giant spoon taller than me.

The flatbed truck it was on was decorated with pink-and-ice-blue fringe. There were two signs on the side of the float. In pastel colors, there was:

SUGAR PLUMS PRESENTS . . .

And in our studio colors:

DANCESTARZ

"It's no gum disease," I said to Lily. "But it'll have to do."

"I think you mean gingivitis," Lily replied with a straight face. We both cracked up.

The other dancers from the studio were milling around the float, excited. They would be walking alongside the float, waving and doing freestyle moves as we moved down the street.

"While the float is moving, you're to stand and wave inside the yogurt cup—but, for safety's sake, do *not* dance," Vanessa instructed us. She told us that at a certain point in the parade, the float would stop, and that was when we'd perform our dance on the flatbed platform.

"Okay, this is hilarious," I said.

"I think we look adorable," Trina said. We all agreed.

"Let me take pictures!" Lily's father came up alongside our float with a camera. "Say cheese! No, say cheesecake-flavored yogurt!"

"Cheese . . . cake!" we all yelled.

I could see one of the employees of the store driving the truck. The marching band ahead of us was playing a fight song, and people twirling batons started throwing them in the air, usually catching them. We all climbed onto our float, ready to go!

The float lurched into motion unexpectedly, and we all lost our balance and knocked into one another. Well, except, apparently, for Megan.

"Ow! Stand firm," Megan commanded. "We're dancers; find your core."

I planted my feet on the ground and steadied myself against the side of the yogurt cup. And we were off! The float moved down the street. It was really fun waving at the people on the sidelines, who waved back at us.

We rolled down the main street of my new town. I'd been spending most of my time in the dance studio, or at home with my mom while she unpacked and set up the new house. I hadn't really gotten out to explore too much. It was weird that this was my new hometown. I waved at people, my new neighbors.

We proceeded by a bank, a cleaning service, and the post office. There was an Indian restaurant my parents had started going to and a yoga place my mom wanted to join. We passed a diner where my dad had taken me for blueberry pancakes once. There was a flower shop, a pizza place that smelled good even from here, and then the library, which reminded me to ask my mom for a library card. And the entrance to what was going to be my new school in a few weeks. *Ack!*

Occasionally, we stopped so that one of the parade participants could perform. Eventually, we turned the corner and could see the road that led to the dance studio and the frozen yogurt store.

"Wave to our home! We love you, DanceStarz!" Trina yelled, and we waved toward the street.

"And Sugar Plums!" Lily cheered.

We passed a few more office buildings and then looped around in a parking lot.

"Look! You can see Energii!" Riley pointed. We all leaned out of the giant cup so we could see their float. You couldn't really miss it. It was an enormous toothbrush and tube of toothpaste, with silver fringe hanging down. The dancers assembled to pose on the float.

"That's town hall. They're going to perform," Riley said.

And we'd get to watch, because from this angle we could see them clearly. Even if they didn't think we were their competition, I wanted to be and to see what we were up against. It looked like they were going to do a large group dance, with the dancers walking on the ground participating too. I particularly wanted to watch the Bells, since they used to dance with my new teammates. I leaned way over the side of the cup to get a good view.

The music echoed across the parking lot, and we watched as Energii started to dance. They began doing some jazz-funk dance moves.

Every single dancer did a kick in perfect unison with the others. Oh, they were good. Then they stopped and pointed to the top of the float. Isabelle and Bella were among the dancers on the top. They all did leg holds that put mine to shame. Their facials were so expressive I could see them from all the way across a parking lot. I understood why the girls had wanted the Bells on their team—and weren't thrilled with me.

"Do you see that?" Megan said quietly. "Do you see what they can do?"

Oh, I'd seen. We all watched their performance silently. I saw Vanessa standing to the side, watching intently as well.

"Well, that was a crowd-pleaser," Lily said. "Can't wait until we get our turn!"

The rest of us groaned.

"What? We're almost as good as that," Lily said. "Come on, we're incredible too!"

I admired her optimism. I knew we were good and separately, *maybe* even incredible. But this team looked like it had been practicing those moves together for a long time. We'd been together for a week and a half. The band in front of us began to march again, and as batons flew, our float lurched forward. I waved at the cheering crowd, but I think we all felt a little subdued after watching Energii's performance.

"High energy!" Megan yelled at us. "Wave and give it your all!"

She was actually right—we had to represent every moment we were here. I livened up and waved at the crowd as we rolled by. And then the float looped around and parked in front of town hall. It was almost our turn to perform!

"The TV station is here!" Lily said, and we all looked to see a local TV news crew, with cameras pointed our way.

"We're going to be on TV!" Megan and Riley jumped up and down, then posed.

The pressure was on.

Vanessa stepped up onto the float.

"Two-minute warning," she said. "Now, this is your first time together as a team. You're here to prove yourselves. You're representing DanceStarz and Sugar Plums, so give it your all! You know what to do."

Megan, Riley, Trina, Lily, and I got in a circle.

"Okay, so this is our first performance ever together," Megan said. "Trina?"

"All right, now's our time to shine!" Trina said.

Every team has one of those inspirational people, and apparently ours was Trina.

"Let's give it one hundred percent," she continued. "Let's do this not just for ourselves but for our team and for DanceStarz and to celebrate our town!"

I did feel a little chill when she said these things. I wanted to give it more than 100 percent, and show everyone what our new team could do!

"Let's do our ritual." Megan had to go and ruin it.

She tapped her nose.

"Wait," I interrupted. They'd never taught us that ritual.

"Ring, ring! Tap, tap, pat, pat!" The Bunheads tapped their noses and patted their knees. Lily and I tried our best to follow it, but we were lost. And then a burst of laughter came from below.

Isabelle and Bella. They were standing at the front of the sidelines, laughing hysterically.

"Look at them! They're still doing the Bells' ritual," Isabelle said loudly.

We all stiffened.

"Did you hear them mocking us?" Megan whispered fiercely. "They're just going to stand there and mock us."

"Haters gonna hate." Lily shrugged.

"We can't let them throw us off our game," I agreed.

"No, you guys don't understand." Megan looked seriously upset now. "We have to kill it. We have to show them. That means: We have to do our routine keeping the jumps."

Wait, what?

"Uh, we're leaving that out, remember?" Lily reminded her.

"The Bells are watching us. Did you even see Energii's routine? Ours is weak without those."

"But Vanessa said not to," I said.

"Didn't you hear her just now?" Megan said. "Vanessa said: 'You know what to do.' That means we do it."

The Bunheads turned to look at me. Megan's gaze pierced

through me. I knew how important it was to her to look good for her rivals. I couldn't blame her. I wanted to look good for my rivals too.

Even if my current rivals happened to be my teammates.

"Okay," I said. "Okay. Let's do it."

"Harper?" Lily looked at me nervously.

Megan wasn't questioning it. She broke from the circle and clapped her hands.

"Take your spots!" Megan shouted. We all jumped out of the yogurt cup and stood in a pyramid formation: Lily and Riley stage right, Trina, Megan, and me stage left. I took a deep breath. I just needed to fight through this.

I could see the line of people along the side of the street, watching us. Including the Bells and, of course, Vanessa.

"Harper!"

And my sister, waving, nudging her way to the front. My parents were trying to keep up with her. *Ack.* I took a deep breath and felt the adrenaline kick in.

Our music started.

Trina and Riley strutted into the center. Lily and I strutted from our side and crossed over. Megan came into the middle and posed. I knew we were looking good. We did a toe-touch jump at the same time, and then a fouetté. . . .

It was time. I prepped for the jumps.

I thought I was doing okay—I really did. Lily later told me I was and that Megan had sped up the moves even from what we had practiced. But regardless, I was the only one who couldn't keep up with them.

Oh, no.

Oh, no.

I jumped in the wrong direction and right into Trina. It happened in slow motion. As we collided, I felt nothing but air underneath my feet and both of us went down . . . down . . . down . . .

Off.

The.

Float.

"It wasn't that bad," my mother told me as she rewrapped the bandage Vanessa had given me to wrap around my banged-up knee.

"Physically," I muttered. Fortunately, I'd just scraped up my knee. What was more injured was my pride. I leaned back on my bed against my fluffy pillow and groaned.

"Oh, it was bad," Hailey said. "You should have seen it; you were like . . ."

Hailey dramatically pretended to fall, her mouth open in horror and her hands pinwheeling wildly in the air. She staggered backward, slid down the bed, and then landed facedown on the carpet.

"It was not that bad, Hailey," my mother repeated. "Minor."

I couldn't even look at Vanessa when she'd come running over. I felt like I'd let her down. And Trina wasn't speaking to me. Lily had been really nice and kept smiling at me at least. The rest of the team had finished the dance—the show must go on!

The doctor from the medical office float checked me out and told me to stay off it for a night because it would bruise. But I'd be fine.

Besides being totally humiliated. What if someone had filmed it and posted it online? My parents had brought me right home, and I'd changed into a cami and shorts and pulled out my fuzzy penguin socks. My mom was taking care of my injury, and my dad offered to go pick up chicken with broccoli for me, but even my favorite food didn't sound appealing. My mom kissed my forehead, and she and Hailey left the room.

My phone blipped. I winced as I reached over to get it. It was Lily.

u ok?

I sent back a thumbs-up emoji. I mean, I *was* okay. Physically. Lily texted back:

good. ☺ Vanessa said she'll talk to us tmw

I cringed. How was I going to face anyone at the studio? I went back on my phone and searched other dance studios in the area. Obviously not Energii. But, like my mom had said, everything else was far away, and I knew my mom was looking for a job, so there was no way she'd be able to drive me that far.

I only had four more years until I got my driver's license. . . .

I couldn't wait four years to dance. I flopped back on my bed. This was hopeless. There was no way I could switch studios. But how could I go to practice tomorrow? I couldn't face the Bunheads, and I certainly couldn't face Vanessa.

I started to cry into my pillow. *Maybe I should just give up dance.*

Wait. What was I saying? *No.* I definitely wasn't going to give up dance. I loved dance. Maybe I could just dance in my room. Maybe I could just never leave my room, so I wouldn't embarrass myself again. My bed would be my stage. My stuffed animals would be my audience. I wouldn't have to deal with people ever again.

There was a knock on my door.

"Please go away!" I yelled, but the door opened anyway.

Mo trotted in and jumped up on my bed. He always hated

when I cried, and he started licking at my old tears. *Oh, Mo, you always know how to make me feel better.*

But Mo doesn't open doors.

"I know you're out there," I called out to my sister.

Hailey came in, holding her hands behind her back.

"I'm not in the mood, sorry," I said, but she disregarded me and jumped on my bed.

"Ouch," I grumbled. "Watch the injured person."

"I am here to cheer you up!" Hailey said. "Since we can't do the Dance Challenge—because you can't dance tonight—and we can't do 'What's in My Cup?' because of my spitting hot sauce . . ."

She held up the canvas bag in which I kept my used stage makeup.

"Blindfolded Makeover Challenge!" Hailey sang out.

"No," I snapped.

"Please," Hailey said. "Just come on. Mom said I could have ice cream if I was nice to you."

She pouted her lower lip and gave me puppy-dog eyes, as did Mo, who stared at me with literal puppy-dog eyes. I knew Hailey was stubborn. I also knew that I liked doing Blindfolded Makeup Challenge.

"Please!" Hailey begged. "I never got to get to the float that was passing out candy, because you fell off yours and we had to leave. You owe me sugar!"

I guess I did owe her a little bit for ruining her parade.

"Okay," I said, and she grinned.

"You just relax while I give you a makeover," she said.

"I'm not sure how relaxing that is," I told her. "But okay."

Hailey took the blindfold and tied it over her eyes.

She picked up a jar of foundation and waved her hand around in the air until she found my face. I started laughing as she scooped a big handful of the foundation and squashed it on my cheeks. "Harper! Don't move your face."

"I—" I shut my mouth quickly as a big brush of face powder went into my mouth. *Ack!* I'd licked the brush. I spat—*bluh, bluh!* She had me close my eyes to put on eyeshadow from a palette—but I don't think she meant to put on the blackest eyeshadow. And it didn't only go on my eyelid. The lip liner application didn't feel promising either.

"And now, the big reveal," she said, pulling off her bandanna. Her eyes widened, and she started laughing. Then she handed me a mirror.

"Oh!" I looked horrifying, and I started laughing. "I look bruised."

"Excuse me, you look fabulous," Hailey said. "I might have been a little too heavy on the eyeshadow. . . ."

"And my lipstick is up my nose." I laughed. "I look ridiculous. Do you want me to do your makeover?"

"Later. I want my ice cream," Hailey said. "I need to wash my hands. They're all gross from your face."

"I need to wash my face." I laughed. "It's all gross from your hands."

"Race you!" Hailey said, and bolted for our bathroom door.

"You want to race an injured person?" I yelled, laughing. "That's so pitiful. Hey, Hails?"

Hailey stuck her head out of the bathroom.

"Thanks for cheering me up," I said. "Seriously."

"As a real thank-you, can I have this lip gloss to keep?"

"Sure," I said. She cheered and fled before I changed my mind. Which I wasn't going to do. She'd been more nice than annoying today. Plus, I had another lip gloss almost exactly the same. Win-win.

My phone blipped with an e-mail. It was from DanceStarz, a group e-mail to the five of us on DanceStarz Squad. I almost ignored it, except it had a ☺ in the subject line and a link. I couldn't resist. I clicked the link.

A television news website loaded, with a video. The

headline said "Town Celebrates Its Anniversary!" I'd half expected it to say, "Bad Dancer Falls off Float."

Oh, no. I can't watch! I put my phone down. I picked it up. I had to watch.

No, no, what if it's horrible?

I can't watch!

Finally, I took a deep breath and pushed the play button. I watched as a newscaster standing in front of the high school marching band began talking into the microphone.

"Our Florida town may be small, a little far from the beach and the theme parks, but boy, can it throw a parade," she said.

After a few minutes, the Sugar Plums giant frozen yogurt cup came into the scene. *Oh, no.* I braced myself. I watched Megan and Trina do their jumps and then it panned to Trina and me as we started our leaps.

Oh no, oh no, here it comes. I winced and put my hands over my eyes, so I could barely peek through my fingers as I watched myself launch into the air and . . .

The camera cut away to a bunch of dogs in cute costumes.

I didn't fall! I can't believe they didn't show my fall! They only showed dogs in cute costumes!

I sat up a little straighter.

I was on the news! I danced on the news! My fall *wasn't* on the news! I laughed. I grabbed my phone to text my parents to come upstairs, so they could see the news clip. But when I picked it up, my video chat went on and I clicked on it to answer without thinking.

"Hi," I said, and then, "Oh!"

Because on my screen was Megan.

"Oh, hey," I said, startled. I was not expecting to see her.

"Hey . . . WHOA!" Megan looked startled too. "You look horrible."

She called to tell me I looked horrible? Then my picture came up on the screen. *Oh yeah, Hailey's makeover.* The black eyeshadow made it look like I had two black eyes. The red lip gloss, like I had a bloody lip. She was right: I looked horrible. I grinned.

"It's—" I opened my mouth to explain.

"So let me just get this out of the way," Megan said. "It was *suggested* that I apologize to you. Even though obviously I wasn't trying to injure you. Obviously, I was just trying to make our routine good enough, and I'm sorry but our routine was really lame before. And you were there when the Bells challenged us, so we *had* to show them our best. Right? RIGHT?"

Megan took a deep breath to calm herself down.

"Okay," I said. That wasn't exactly an apology, but I got where she was coming from. There was an awkward pause.

"All right, that's done," Megan said, perking up. "Did you see us on the news?"

"Yeah," I said. "Fortunately, they only showed the good parts."

"See, when you do what I tell you, we end up on TV!" Megan smiled brightly.

"Um. When I did what you told me, I *fell off the float*," I replied.

"True." Megan tried again. "All right. How about this: When we work together as a team, things can go great."

"Yeah," I said, surprised she'd admitted it. "Well said."

"Actually, that's what Vanessa said when she told me to call you and apologize." Megan rolled her eyes.

"Look. I know you'd rather have the Bells here," I said. "But I want to be on a team that wants me—"

"What team wants you?" Megan suddenly interrupted. "Energii?"

"Huh?" She obviously was misunderstanding me.

"I knew it!" Megan looked enraged. "Energii called you! They're trying to steal you!"

"What?" I sputtered.

"They saw you on the news," Megan kept going. "They saw your turns and wanted you, didn't they?!"

I smiled a little bit.

"Did you just compliment my turns?" I asked her.

"Well," Megan said. "That's obvious. I mean, I knew you were good when you did that move over me during the lyrical improv."

Well, well, well. I was pleased with this progress.

"So," she continued, "I can see why Energii would try to steal you and—"

"MEGAN!" I interrupted her. "Energii did NOT call me! I am NOT going to leave DanceStarz! That is, if . . ."

I paused for dramatic effect.

". . . we really can work together as a team," I said. "All of us."

"Well, obvs." Megan tried to sound casual about it. "I mean, if you leave, then Lily will probably leave, and we won't have enough people for a team. The next-best dancer is Carlee, and she cries if she doesn't get a solo. Do you cry when you don't get a solo?"

"No," I answered.

"See? We need you," Megan said.

I did like to be needed. Even more than that, I wanted to be wanted on the team.

"Also," Megan said, "will you show me how you spot when you do your turns?"

"Will you stop moving my dance bag at the cubbies?" I asked.

"I don't—" Megan wasn't expecting that.

I raised an eyebrow at her.

"Fine, I'll tell Riley to stop moving it," she said.

"Then I accept your apology," I said firmly.

"Anyway, I hope your face looks better soon," Megan said. "It's pretty bad. Looks like it's going to be a while, though."

"Yeah." I tried not to smile as I admired myself in the video. Hailey really had made me look wrecked. "I'm going to hope for a miraculous recovery."

"Wow, you had a miraculous recovery," Megan said.

The miracle was makeup remover wipes. I grinned.

"Your face looks almost as good as it did before," Megan told me.

Almost?

Megan had gotten out of her car exactly the same time as I had. I had a feeling that wasn't a coincidence and that she'd been waiting for me. My mom dropped back to let me walk ahead with Megan through the parking lot.

"Anyway," she said. "Are we still cool?"

"Yeah," I said.

"And you're going to tell Vanessa that, right? She'll want us to have worked things out and stick together and—"

"YES. I'll tell her!" I cut her off. I realized she was nervous about seeing Vanessa too. I was nervous enough without adding any more pressure.

When we walked into the lobby, it was the usual chaos of parents talking and little kids in leotards running around.

Some girls turned around to look at us.

"Megan!" One of the girls smirked at me. "Crazy parade, huh?"

Megan and I looked at each other.

"Late to class!" She waved the girl off.

"Thanks," I said.

"We're sticking together." Megan shrugged. Then she glanced toward Vanessa's door. "Remember, Vanessa might be watching us."

Well, even if this "make Harper feel better" was all for show, it was working.

A boy in ballet warm-ups looked over and laughed. Megan shot him a mean look. Then she grabbed my hand and we ran into our classroom together.

When we burst into the room, our other teammates were already there, stretching. They all looked at us—and looked totally shocked.

Megan and I glanced down and realized we were still holding hands.

"What?" Megan snapped. "Team bonding, blah, blah. Continue on."

We dropped our hands. Megan and I pulled off our street clothes so we matched the rest of the team, wearing our black leotard and shell-pink tights, with our hair in buns at the crowns of our heads. Megan went over to sit with the Bunheads, and I went by Lily.

"Team bonding?" Lily raised an eyebrow.

"Well, I had to—"

"No, no, I get it," Lily said. "We need to be a team. It's good."

"Thanks, Lily."

"How's your knee?" She looked down at my leg.

"It's just a little stiff," I told her. "The doctor said I can dance on it, though."

"Good," she said. She lowered her voice to almost a whisper. "You'd better be good, or I'll be stuck alone with the Bunheads."

I looked at the Bunheads. Trina and Megan were stretching. Riley saw me and rolled her eyes.

Okay. Riley wasn't quite up to the speed on the whole getting-along thing. I ignored her. I had more important things to worry about.

Vanessa came into the room and looked at all of us.

"Good," she said. "You're all here. Together. That's the way I like to see you. Together as a team."

"That's us!" Megan said extra brightly. "A team!"

"I'd like to talk to Harper alone for a moment," Vanessa said.

Here we go.

I followed Vanessa out of the studio and around the corner to her office. I was so anxious to get it over with, I barely made it into the office before I blurted it out.

"I'm sorry I fell off the float."

"Anyone can fall. It's what led to that situation that we need to discuss," she said sternly. She shut her office door and sat down in a chair behind her desk. She motioned for me to sit down too. "I've already discussed it with the other girls and their parents. All of you disregarded what I had instructed, and that led to a safety issue. Someone got hurt. We can't have that here in the studio."

I nodded.

"I made an exception for you with your late audition," she said. "Did I make a mistake?"

I shook my head no. Tears started welling up in my eyes.

"I was just trying to prove myself to everybody," I said softly. "I thought if I could just get that combination right, I would impress everyone."

I slumped miserably down in my seat. Instead of proving myself, I'd done the opposite.

"You should have told me you felt that way," Vanessa said, a little more kindly this time. "Next time, I need you to speak up. Now that I know what the issue is, let's take care of it. Let's schedule a private lesson. Say, fifteen minutes after pointe class."

"Okay," I said. A private with her was actually a reward, not the punishment I'd been worried about. I would show her how hard I could work. "Sure."

Vanessa stood up and looked me straight in the eye.

"Harper, you're not the only person who is new here. I am new here too. We both have something to prove. I get that." And then she smiled. "And we both are exceptional at what we do. So let's get it done."

"Okay!" I nodded. "I will. *I will!*"

Suddenly, I felt really pumped to get it done.

"How's your knee? Well enough to dance?" she asked me, and I nodded. "Let's go back to class."

We went silently back into the dance studio. The other girls were already at the barre, working on moves, and they all looked up.

"Pointe shoes on," Vanessa said to me.

I ran to get my pointe shoes. Then Lily grabbed my arm

and pulled me to the corner of the room, away from the Bunheads and Vanessa. We sat down to put on our shoes.

"Hey," Lily said quietly. "How did that go?"

"I think okay," I said, pulling on my shoe.

"Well, it wasn't your fault," Lily said.

"It's not *not* my fault," I said.

"It's our whole team's fault," Lily said, lacing up her ribbons. "I don't blame you. It's kind of hard to say no to three people who have been here forever."

"Yeah," I sighed. "Hopefully, we can just be a team from now on."

"Yeah, right. The Bunheads want their chance to rule now that the Bells are gone," Lily said.

"Actually, I talked to Megan last night and—"

Vanessa clapped her hands.

"To the barre!" she ordered. "We've wasted enough time on shenanigans. I'm going to work you hard today."

I hurriedly tied the ribbons around each ankle in a knot and tucked them in neatly.

"Time to suffer," Lily whispered. "Ugh, pointe."

I actually loved ballet technique class and had especially since I'd gone on pointe. Dancers have a love/hate relationship with going on pointe. When I was little, I couldn't wait for the rite of passage when my teacher told me I was ready to go *en pointe*. It seemed like something only the older, "real" ballerinas were able to do. When I was eleven, that magical moment came! Getting my first pair of pointe shoes and learning to support my entire body on my toes was so exciting, and I felt like I was finally on the level of the older dancers.

I still loved the feeling of pulling on my pointe shoes. Dancing in them . . . love/hate. They're not the most comfortable at first—actually, painful. It takes a while to get used to them. But you feel like a real ballerina, able to spin and twirl on your toes. You feel strong and powerful. I needed anything to make me feel strong and powerful these days.

Also, the classes are *hard*. Which actually would be a good thing right now. I would have to focus and do my movements precisely, so I couldn't think about anything else. Not the parade, the Bunheads, the Bells, or my move. Just dancing.

We all placed our hands on the barre, barely gripping it, and it quivered slightly as we started to move. We did the positions and moved to pliés.

"And plié," Vanessa commanded. "Remember to stand up straight and engage your core muscles. Plié combos! Harper! Watch those knees!"

We transitioned to larger movements of the leg, circling

them in rond de jambes, then bending them in fondus. For the next half hour, my thoughts were solely about my body movements. The tempo of the music got faster, and my muscles began to burn.

"Excellent pointed feet, Harper," Vanessa said.

She walked around, giving corrections.

"Riley, sloppy feet! Trina, you're wobbly! Lily, your turnout! Poor turnout breaks a dancer's lines!"

I focused. I focused on making every little movement perfect over and over again, so I would be able to depend on muscle memory later, when I was performing. I got lost in the dance moves. I channeled all of the stress and anger from the weekend into my body.

"Very nice technique," Vanessa said. "Everyone watch Harper's feet!"

When class ended, I ached but in a good way.

"Megan, Riley, and Trina: Come with me when your shoes are off," Vanessa said.

The Bunheads made a *yikes* face at each other and followed Vanessa out of the room.

"Well, at least class ended okay," Lily said when the door shut. "The Bunheads are probably going to get in trouble with Vanessa."

"I just want to put it behind us," I said.

"Hey, you had to suffer." Lily pointed to my knee. "They need to suffer."

"Speaking of suffering." I changed the subject. "That class was intense."

"So painful," Lily said as we put our stuff in our bags.

"The doctor gave me a new muscle rub if you want it." I reached into my bag to look for it.

"I meant all the corrections Vanessa gave me. Turnout! Ribs in! Shoulders down! I've been taking intensive ballet forever and I can't get my turnout right. You're so good at footwork and technique."

"My teachers have told me I have good feet," I said, holding out my foot. "High arches, so I can hyperextend and all that. I can't really take credit for it."

"Okay, but that's not it. You're also really focused," Lily said. "You're really standing out already."

I laughed.

"Yeah, by falling off the float!" I said.

"Yeah, I'm blending so much I'm invisible," Lily said quietly. "At least you got to be on the news."

Oh. I hadn't really thought about it like that.

"You know the news showed you because of your amazing

twirls," she said. "And you won the freestyle dance-off and you got a ton of likes."

"Oh! Well! I guess it's kind of cool," I said.

"It's *really* cool!" Lily smiled at me. "Go get some good attention and then share some with me, okay? Hey, can you go to Sugar Plums now? You don't have class after this, right?"

"Oh," I said. "I'm really sorry, but I can't. I have to meet with Vanessa."

"About the parade? Again? Is something wrong?"

"No, no!" I assured her. I was going to tell her that was a private lesson to help me with these tricky steps from our routine, but then I felt stupid. Here was Lily, thinking I was this special dancer, getting the attention, who won the dance-off and was on the news. I didn't want to remind her, or anyone—or myself—of my failures.

I took a deep breath. I just needed to master the dance moves and forget the big mess I'd caused—and be the great dancer that truly deserved all of the attention.

16

Trust me, I would have rather gone to Sugar Plums with Lily.

I walked into Studio C. I was already warmed up from pointe, so I just did a few twirls to loosen up. It was weird to be in an empty studio. I looked up at the video camera and realized that everyone in the lobby could see into the room. The last thing I wanted was the Bunheads to look up and see me messing up my steps with Vanessa. I found the remote control and clicked a button so the red light turned off.

Then Trina walked in.

"Oh, hey!" I said. "Are you looking for the other Bunheads?"

"No, Megan and Riley have a tumbling private in Studio B," she said.

"Well, uh, I think this room is reserved."

"It is!" Trina said brightly. "For us!"

Huh? Vanessa walked in the door.

"Good. You're both here," Vanessa said.

"Trina needs to work on the tricky steps too?" I was confused. Trina had actually nailed those steps.

"No, no. Trina is going to work with you," Vanessa said.

"I thought, um, *you* were going to help me?" I asked hopefully.

"Trina will help you. She is good at teaching and explaining things," Vanessa said.

"Vanessa has me work with a lot of the little kids." Trina nodded. "I assist with the minis."

The minis. Great. She teaches the minis—and me. Okay, in my old studio, if someone couldn't get the choreography, it would be no big deal for someone to help them. But here, it was tricky. The Bunheads didn't want me here, and I already felt stupid enough trying to keep up.

To have Vanessa make Trina tutor me like a mini . . . That was pitiful. Oh no, the Bunheads must think this is hilarious.

"But—"

"Trina is very patient," Vanessa cut me off. "Take your time. This studio is unused until four."

With that, she left. So. Vanessa thought I'd need a lot of time and patience. Just like the minis.

This was humiliating.

"Okay!" Trina said, looking at me. "Is that the music remote?"

"No, it's the monitor. I turned it off so nobody in the lobby can see us." I gave her a pointed look. As in her friends. As in the Bunheads. Well, at least the other two, who weren't in the room actually watching me mess up.

"Then it's time to sweat, sparkle, and shine!" she said brightly. "That's my new signature saying before I teach. Do you think it's good? Or stupid? You think it's stupid, don't you?"

"Uh, no?" I said.

"It's the first time I've ever used it. It sounded good in my head, but it felt kind of silly when I actually said it out loud." Trina bit her lip.

"You?" I couldn't help saying. "The only one stupid here is me. I can't get those tricky steps. Your saying isn't stupid."

"Oh, goody! Well then, it's sweat, sparkle, and shine time!" Trina said happily. "Show me what you got."

"Well, as you know, I keep ending up the wrong way." I

went into the quick moves and the tricky steps, screwing up as always.

"Back up a few steps and show me how you're going into it," Trina said. "Let's break it down."

She watched me dance and her eyebrows furrowed. I felt myself get more and more uptight every time I goofed it up. Finally, I just stopped.

"I'm not getting it," I said, frustrated.

"You need to re—"

"Relax, I know, I know. My teachers always tell me to relax," I said.

"I was going to say remember to look at the spot so you don't get confused," Trina said. "I was not saying 'relax.' Ugh, I hate when people tell me to relax. It always makes me feel even more tense."

"I know, right? It makes it worse," I agreed. "I mean, I'll relax when I get things right."

"You do need to get out of your head, though." Trina frowned. "Here, let's just break down the steps and you can memorize them without overthinking it."

We went to the center of the floor.

"Okay, let's just start with the first eight counts here, and we will keep adding on bit by bit," Trina suggested. We tried that. Trina's advice was actually really helpful. I tried it through again, with a stumble but a little smoother. She had me practice over and over again.

"You are really patient. And a good teacher. You really broke down the steps and explained to me," I told her. I realized I'd judged her. She was pretty smart in a way I hadn't thought about before.

"Thanks!" she said happily. "That's why I get to teach the little kids."

"Well, now I just feel stupid," I said.

"Why?" Trina said.

"Because, like you said, you teach little kids. I'm not a little kid. I'm on the select team. I should be able to do this choreo," I said.

"But you can do other things," Trina said. "Like your pirouettes. I don't feel stupid that I can't do that."

She had a point. The Bunheads had just made me feel so embarrassed that I couldn't do their signature move.

But they couldn't do my signature move, could they?

Trina's phone beeped.

"My sister is almost here," Trina said. Then she looked at me. "Hey, where do you live?"

I told her.

"That's on our way. Do you want a ride home from my sister?" Trina asked.

That actually could be good. When I'd told my mom I was staying late, she'd told me I would have to wait because she had to get her errands done first. This way, I wouldn't have to wait around for her. I texted my mom, and I answered her questions about how long her sister had been driving and other mother-type safety things.

"My mom said yes and thanks," I told Trina.

The door opened.

"Oh!" Riley came in. "I didn't know anyone was in here."

Just when I thought things were going okay. I'd been hoping the Bunheads wouldn't have to know about this tutoring.

"What are you guys doing in here?" Riley asked.

"Us?" Trina asked. "What are *you* doing in here?"

"Vanessa just asked me to hang up some flyers around the studio." Riley held up some papers in her hand.

"And I was looking for you!" Trina said. "So yay! I found you!"

"You knew I was going to be coming into this room?" Riley was genuinely confused.

"She did." I nodded vigorously. "I was just here practicing and she came in and asked if you had been here yet!"

"I just had a feeling!" Trina said. "Sometimes I'm good like that. I wanted to see the flyer!"

"You knew I was going to have to pass out flyers?" Riley asked.

"She did." I nodded again. "She asked if you'd been here to pass out flyers!"

"That is so spooky," Riley said.

Surprisingly, she fell for it.

"Hey, what's on the flyer?" Trina asked her.

"A hip-hop workshop!" Riley sounded excited.

I remembered that she had said hip-hop was her favorite. I looked at the flyer.

HIP-HOP WORKSHOP!
with Guest Choreographer
George J. from Miami

It was scheduled for Wednesday, right before our rehearsal. I definitely hoped I could go. I hadn't been able to take a hip-hop class since we'd moved here. Even though I wasn't the best at hip-hop, I loved the high-energy fun in class.

"Well, now that I've found you, you can go finish up your posters!" Trina said.

"Okay." Riley shrugged and left.

"Thanks for covering for me," I said.

"I always give my students privacy." Trina smiled. "Well, I mean, usually they have their moms with them because they're like five or six years old, but—"

"I got it." I sighed. At least she hadn't given me away to the other Bunheads.

I hung back as Trina went out into the lobby. I noticed some of the younger girls saying hi to her and running up to give her hugs. I had a new respect for her teaching skills and her patience. I needed some more of that with my little sister sometimes.

When she went to the front door, she turned to look to see if I was coming. I quickly went outside to her sister's car.

"Hi!" Her sister had the window down and smiled. "I'm Alexis."

"I'm Harper. Thanks for taking me home," I said.

"No problem; we have to go that way anyway," she said.

I got into the backseat and Trina got in the other side—and slid into the back next to me. I thought it was a little weird that she didn't sit in the front.

Then the front door opened.

"Hiiii, Alexis!" Megan said, and leaned over to give Trina's sister an air kiss. "Hi, Trina! Hi—"

Megan was startled.

"You're not Riley," she said.

"No. I'm not," I said.

Just then the door next to me opened and Riley jumped in—right on my lap.

"Ack!" we both said.

"What are *you* doing here?" Riley asked. "Are you every-where?"

"Riley! That sounded rude!" Alexis glared at her, and Riley looked embarrassed.

"I mean, uh," Riley stammered. "Uh. Skooch over."

I slid over to give her room too.

"Alexis, that is so nice of you to give Harper a ride," Megan said. "And Trina is being such a good teammate, just like Vanessa told us to do. Right, Riley?"

"Right," Riley muttered.

"Smile, everyone!" Megan said, holding up her phone. "I'll add this to my story!"

"Hey, it's DanceStarz Squad!" Megan cheered into the phone. "Hanging out with Alexis, our fave high school cheer-leader! And Harper, our new Squad member bestie. Wave to my fans, Harper!"

"Uh." I waved awkwardly. Bestie? Megan was really play-ing this up.

"And me, Rileeeey!" Riley sang out, waving wildly.

"Oh, I already stopped filming," Megan said. "There, I posted it."

"Buckle up, people," Alexis said, and started to drive.

"Harper, wave to my fans!"

Megan's voice came out of Riley's phone. Riley was watching the video, and I peered over her shoulder. Yup, my face was front and center. I noticed it was tagged "#DanceStarz." Megan definitely wanted Vanessa to see her "team bonding" efforts.

"You totally cut me off," Riley whispered to me, like it was my fault.

"Hey, Riley! Did you know Harper lives right near you?" Alexis said, as if that were a good thing. Riley didn't seem too thrilled. "So, what class did you guys have?"

"Um . . . dance class!" Trina did not cover up our secret too well. Fortunately, Megan was more than happy to talk over her.

"I think she figured that out." Megan laughed. "First, we had ballet technique, and then Trina waited for us while Riley and I had a tumbling private," Megan said. "I'm working on my round-off to back layout."

"That's great," Alexis said. "If you do cheer in high school, they're going to love that you can do one."

Megan sat up straight and smiled. We pulled out of the parking spot and drove past Sugar Plums, and then out onto the main road.

"Where do you go to school, Harper?" Alexis asked.

"I'm starting at South," I told her.

"Riley goes to South!" Trina said. "Megan and I go to North."

"Oooh. You're our rivals," Alexis said, in a teasing voice. "Wait till football season."

"Ugh, I wish I went to North," Riley grumbled. "So much better."

"Truth." Megan laughed.

"Don't listen to the haters," Alexis said. "South is a good school too. Don't tell my cheer squad I said that, though. Boo, South!"

"Well, we have better colors, Harper." Riley turned to me. "*We're* red and white. They're green and yellow."

"Gold," Megan shot back. "Green and *gold*."

"Eh, it's still pretty ugly," Alexis admitted, laughing. "Oh, so Isabelle will be at your school, Harper."

She will? I looked at the Bunheads for confirmation.

"Yeah." Riley's face dropped. "She will. She's a grade older, though."

"At least you'll get to see her," Megan said.

"Aw, you miss her," Alexis said. "It is a little strange not driving those Bells around anymore."

"I know," Megan whined. "It's not the same without them."

"That's a little sad," Alexis said. "But now your team won't get stale. You have what Harper and the other new girl bring to the table."

"Her name's Lily," I said. "She's super athletic and really good at tumbling."

"And Harper is really good at technique," Trina said, surprising me. "I think it's going to help our technical scores."

"Thanks," I said honestly. That was nice of her to say.

"But I don't know how can we even compete with Energii...." Megan let out a huge sigh and slumped in her seat.

"Sometimes it's good to have rivals who challenge you," Alexis said. "Like when we play South, we get all woke!"

"Sometimes rivals are just annoying," Riley said, and I realized she was directing that at me.

When we pulled into the driveway, I thanked Alexis for the ride and turned to Riley.

"See you at the hip-hop workshop," I said nicely. She was right. I *would* be everywhere.

"SASS!"

George, the guest choreographer, had introduced himself with high energy, high-fiving each of us as we walked in the door.

"I want to see some sass!" he was now shouting out. "Are you going to show me sass?"

"YESS!" people called back.

The music was already pumping, loud with a heavy bass. The workshop was packed with about thirty people. We got into three lines. I'd originally stood next to Lily, but in the shuffle, she was now a few people away.

"Spread out into lines!"

The Bunheads went right up in front of the teacher. Hip-hop wasn't my best, so I thought about hiding in the middle.

But I was determined. We needed to stick together as a team. I motioned to Lily that we should go up front—and not just up front, but by the Bunheads. I hurried up and slid into the front line.

"Warm up!" George announced.

I looked to the side to see Lily, but she wasn't there. I could see her in the mirror a row back on the other side. I felt bad she hadn't seen me tell her I'd come up front. Well, it was just warm-ups, so I'd catch her afterward.

I watched myself in the mirror as I did neck rolls. I was wearing a white tee, a red plaid shirt tied around my waist, my new black leggings with the mesh sides, and black-and-white sneakers. I had my hair in a very high ponytail, which I flipped as I did neck rolls.

First, we did toe touches side to side, then put our hands on our hips and rocked back and forth, then did step touches, and finally, jumping jacks.

"We're going to start a combo now," George said. "Let's break down the first block."

I looked for Lily. She was standing alone near the back corner away from the crowd. I ran over to stand next to her.

"This teacher is fun," I said, and she nodded. She seemed distracted, so I guessed I was interrupting her focus. I turned forward and focused as well.

"I want to see lots of attitude!" he yelled. "Work your coolness."

"I don't have a lot of coolness," I joked to Lily. She looked at me and smiled, but only a little.

Hmmm. Before I could say anything, the music started from the top.

George walked through us and yelled, "Hit, hit, boom, boom! Yes!"

He stood in front of Lily: "Sharp accents, yes! That's it!"

I smiled at Lily, but she was just doing her body roll.

"Yay, he called you out!" I said to her, but she body-rolled the other way.

I knew something was up with her for sure. When we were done with the combo, everyone clapped and cheered. Lily still wasn't looking my way.

"Freezes!" George called out. Freezes are break dancing moves where you freeze your body in the middle of a move. It also felt like what Lily was doing to me: freezing me out.

"Beginners to the front and I'll teach you the basics," he said. "Everyone else, spread out."

Lily went to the back of the room, almost in a corner. I ran to stand next to her.

"Handstand freeze!" George called out.

He flipped himself into a handstand and froze his feet for an insanely long time. We clapped and cheered him on.

Then it was our turn to try them. This resulted in some solid handstands with legs bent in a variety of ways. I looked over to Lily. She caught my eye and glanced away.

"Lily!" I said over the music. "Are you mad at me?"

"Well, yeah," Lily said. As if it were obvious.

She *was* mad at me? I fell over in shock. Okay, she was mad. What had I done to make her mad? I needed to know.

"Why are you—?"

"Baby freeze!" George called out, demonstrating.

I didn't get to finish my sentence. Okay, baby freeze. A baby freeze was a beginning freeze, but still a challenge. We both squatted down. I put my weight on my arms and rested the top of my head on the floor. I kicked my feet up toward the ceiling. We maneuvered our legs into crooked positions and froze.

"Why are you mad at me?" I finally asked her, my voice

cracking a little from the effort it took to talk while I was twisted like a pretzel.

"Because you lied to me," Lily said.

"What? When did I lie to you?!"

"Shoulder freeze!" George called out.

Ugh! Lily turned away from me as she went into a shoulder freeze. She was giving me the cold shoulder, literally. I needed to get this taken care of. I got up and went around to the other side of Lily.

"What are you talking about?" I asked her, positioning myself into a shoulder freeze. Ugh. The only part of your body touching the floor was your shoulder, and it was really hard to hold the pose for a long time. At least for me!

"Yesterday, when I asked you to come to Sugar Plums, you said you had to meet with Vanessa. You weren't rehearsing." Her voice cracked, but it wasn't with effort. I could tell she was really upset.

"No, I was rehearsing—" I protested.

"I saw the video," Lily said. "You were with your Squad *besties!*"

Oh. OH. I fell over again, but Lily was holding that pose strong.

"Ohhhh! I wasn't lying. I—"

"I mean, it makes sense," Lily cut me off. "They're all talented and you're really talented and I'm a nobody here, so you'd rather hang out with the you-know-whos over me."

"That's not true!" I said.

"Chair freeze!" George yelled.

Lily spun around on the ground and lifted herself into a chair freeze. Ugh, I was awful at these. I put my hands down, then my head, and kicked my feet up in the air. Once I got settled in, I talked to her again.

"I wasn't hanging out with them—" I looked at Lily, upside down, and saw that she was starting to cry a little bit.

"Harper," Lily cut me off. "They're our team, so of course you should hang with them. I just didn't want to be lied to about it. And it stinks to be left out. That was savage."

I fell over.

"Keep trying!" George yelled back at me. *Augh.* I flipped upside down again into, actually, a pretty decent chair freeze and confessed.

"I was only getting a ride home from Trina's sister," I said. "After I had *secret* tutoring from Trina for those harder moves from the routine. I'd thought Vanessa was going to tutor me. Trust me, I was shocked when it was Trina. Vanessa asked her because she's so good at teaching the minis that she thought she could help me."

Lily's mouth moved into a grin for a second. She shifted her hands to stay in the freeze.

"Exactly," I said. "Totally humiliating. And, of course, I didn't want the Bunheads to find out and embarrass me."

"Oh," Lily said. "But wait—you were *with* the Bunheads."

"Only because Trina's sister gave everyone a ride home," I said. "I promise."

"And the *besties*?" Lily still looked skeptical.

"I think that was for Vanessa to see," I told her. "I wasn't lying on purpose, and I wasn't leaving you out."

"Oh. OH. I was so sad." Lily sniffled. "But that makes sense."

I fell over with relief, and also because my arms felt like they were going to fall off.

"Did we just have our first fight upside down?" I asked Lily.

"Yes! That's pretty weird." Lily laughed and then sniffled. "And I'm totally crying upside down, aren't I?"

"Yes, also weird," I said. "Your tears are running up your forehead."

We both started laughing as she flipped right side up. George was complimenting other people, who, I couldn't believe it, were still doing their freezes.

"I'm sorry," Lily said. "We should be with them; they're our team."

"Look, if they get mean again, then we shouldn't take it," I said. "But Trina actually was really nice yesterday. Megan is at least acting nice because she has to. Riley . . . well. Hopefully, they'll just get used to the idea of us being here."

"That would be good." Lily sighed. "Do you think we can get them to stop hiding my backpack?"

"Oh, they did that to you, too?" I shook my head. "Yes. Yes, I'm sure we can."

"Excellent freezes!" George called out, and he turned off the music. "Now it's time to freestyle. Scatter!"

We looked at each other, with the same idea. I followed Lily as we wove through the dancers to go to the front of the class, standing with the Bunheads as George came to the front of the room.

"Hey, teammates!" I said to them. They didn't have time to respond one way or the other, because George came right in front of us and gave us high fives.

"Hip-hop is different from many forms of dance, because it's often improvisational," George told us. "So let's freestyle!"

The lights went off, and colorful strobe lights came flashing across the room.

"So cool!" Lily high-fived me as music came on with an

intense beat. We all started freestyling. Popping, locking, body-rolling, and hinging.

"Your accents are sharp!" George came over and told Megan.

"Go, Megan!" I danced over to her and high-fived her. She looked at me, a little confused.

Lily got on the floor and started windmilling, hands on the floor, kicking her legs around in a circle.

"Whoo!" a couple people yelled to her. When she jumped up, George ran over and high-fived her.

This was fun. When the song ended, everyone cheered.

"You all did great work today," George said. "I hope I see you all again soon!"

Lily flashed me the peace sign. That gave me an idea. I looked at the clock. We still had ten minutes until DanceStarz Squad rehearsal.

"I'll be there in a minute," I told Lily. When I left the room, instead of going to Studio B for rehearsal, I went out to the lobby. I went over to the big couch, where my mom was with the other mothers.

"Excuse me." I smiled at everyone. Then I leaned down and asked my mother a question. She nodded. I ran back into Studio B. The Bunheads and Lily were sitting on the floor either changing out of their sneakers from hip-hop or stretching. Vanessa wasn't there yet. Perfect.

"Okay!" I said.

Everyone looked up at me.

"Okay!" I stalled, to get my nerve up. "I want to say something. First, can whoever keeps moving my bag please stop? Thank you."

I didn't look to see the Bunheads' reactions. If I was going to move forward, I needed to be all in. I checked my phone and saw the text from my mom.

"Second, we have a competition in two days. I think we need some team bonding," I said to everyone. "So I want to invite everyone over to my house after practice. Everyone's parents said yes. Well, Trina, I don't know about yours yet."

"I'll text my sister!" Trina said cheerfully.

I looked at the other Bunheads.

"Okay," Megan said.

"Okay," Riley repeated.

"Okay, then!" I said, trying not to show my relief. Next, there was one other thing I wanted to do.

"Don't you guys think we should come up with a new team ritual?" I said. "Then we can do it before our first competition dance."

Like one without ringing bells, ahem . . .

"But we've always—" Megan started, but to my surprise it was Riley who interrupted her.

"She's right," Riley agreed. "We can set a whole new tradition for DanceStarz Squad by ourselves. Then the Bells won't make fun of us for using their ideas."

"Truuue," Megan said thoughtfully. "Okay, let's do it. I actually already have some ideas—"

"Like these?" Trina jumped in. She did jazz hands, then shimmied. Then she patted her head and stomach simultaneously, twirled around, and finished by plugging her nose and doing the swim.

Everyone was silent for a moment.

"No," Megan said. "Not exactly like those."

"Are you sure? Look how fun it is!" Trina started doing the same routine again, as the door opened and Vanessa came into the studio. She watched Trina shimmy, then pat her head and her stomach.

"Do I even want to know what is going on?" Vanessa asked us, continuing to watch Trina do the swim.

"We're not happy with our competition routine," I said. "So Megan choreographed a new one for us. Do you like it?"

"Wait, WHAT?" Megan burst out. "No! Vanessa, that's not true!"

"Megan, I know it's not true." Vanessa smiled. "I do have a sense of humor."

"Well." Megan stumbled over her words. "Oh. Okay, then."

"They're my ideas for the ritual!" Trina explained to her.

"Vanessa, is it all right if we make up a new ritual?" I asked her.

"I think that's a great idea," Vanessa said. "Let's run through the dance a few times and then we'll save some time so you can create one. And, in other announcements . . ." Vanessa paused dramatically. "Your costumes have arrived."

"OUR COSTUMES!" Riley shrieked. Then she looked around, embarrassed. "Sorry, it's my favorite thing."

She didn't have to apologize! We were all excited to see our first costumes.

Vanessa opened the box and pulled out one to show to us. We would all wear matching costumes, for unity, she told us.

It was gorgeous. A sparkly top with a dramatic skirt, which would all look amazing on stage.

"I'm so excited for our first competition!" Trina said.

"Then let's dance so we can bring home our first trophy," Vanessa said. "Let's get to work."

One of Vanessa's assistants came in carrying a huge box

and put it down in front of us. Vanessa reached into the box and pulled out—

"OUR JACKETS!" we all screamed.

Our team jackets were here! They were athletic material with an ombré starting at the top going from white to pink to a darker pink. And on the back:

DANCESTARZ SQUAD!

Our logo was in shimmery gold.

We all put on our jackets and started dancing around, showing them off and checking ourselves out in the mirror.

Trina danced by me, and I waved jazz hands at her. She joined me, and we both did her next move—shimmying. Lily and Riley caught on as we patted our heads and rubbed our stomachs. Megan rolled her eyes but joined us doing the swim.

"Does this mean we're using my new ritual?" Trina asked.

"NO!" we all blurted out.

Even Vanessa.

"So how was practice?" my mother asked us.

My mom had offered to drive us all to my house after practice. By "us," I meant our whole team. I sat in the front passenger seat next to my mom.

"Our dance is looking really good," Megan said. "Harper is doing great."

I wasn't sure if she was just saying that because she was talking to my mom, but regardless I was pretty happy with how I was doing. We had incorporated the tricky moves, but after Trina's help and extra practice, I felt pretty comfortable. Plus, thankfully Vanessa had placed me in the back for that part of the dance. There were only five of us, so it wasn't like I could hide.

But while the rest of us were doing those moves, Riley was going to be featured in the middle doing a big handstand.

My mom was smiling. She was so mom-pleased I'd finally invited people over and that they were saying nice things about me.

She asked me to grab her phone and to text my sister's babysitter now that we were almost home. I added a message to pass along to my sister, too.

When we went into my house, Trina squealed. My dog rushed at them, wagging his tail so hard it almost wriggled off. The girls bent down to pet him.

"That's Mo," I told them.

"He's so cute," Riley said. "I want a dog so bad."

Mo was so excited he was flinging himself from person to person.

"Why don't you take them to your room and I'll get some snacks ready down here," my mom said.

"Can Mo come too?" Riley cooed.

"Yeah," I said. "Come on, Mo!"

We went upstairs and I pushed open my bedroom door.

"Your room is so cute!" Lily said.

"It's still in progress," I said. "But thanks."

"It's so neat," Trina noted.

"Yeah, I'm kind of an organization queen," I said.

"Ooh, you like him too?" Megan pointed to the big poster of my favorite actor from his most recent movie.

Riley sat down on my lavender fluffy chair and patted it for Mo to jump onto her lap.

The other girls looked around at my pictures and my awards.

"Aw, is that your old team?" Lily looked at our team picture from last year. "Wow, that's a huge squad."

"I know, it's been really different," I said. "But I was with them since I was three, so I was used to it."

"Don't you miss them?" Trina asked me.

"Yeah, a lot." I sighed. "They just did their first competition over the weekend."

It had been so weird to see my old team on social media without me. They had placed well in groups, and my friends had placed in top five and top ten in solo and individuals. I couldn't help but wonder how I would have done if I'd been there.

"Did they win?" Megan asked me.

"Our group came in second," I said.

"They would have won if you were there, I bet," Lily said.

I smiled at her.

"You had a solo at nationals? Wait, you won a technical award?" Megan pointed to one of my trophies.

"Yeah," I said proudly.

"Harper, that's so cool!" Lily said, going over to look at it. She held it out so the other girls could see it.

Megan and Riley admired my jewelry, Trina my stuffed animals, and Lily just bounced around on my bed with me. It felt a little awkward to have them checking everything out, but mostly it felt good to have people over in my room, finally. Plus, I was proud of my stuff!

"HARPER!"

My sister was yelling up to me from her room. I smiled. As I'd asked her, she'd put something together for me that I was hoping would be fun. We all went down the hall to Hailey's room, and I knocked on her bedroom door.

"Welcome to 'Does Hailey Think You Can Dance?!'" Hailey called out dramatically into her unplugged karaoke microphone.

"You look so glamorous," Megan told her.

Hailey did. She was wearing one of my dance costumes—with my permission. It was a dark blue spaghetti-strap dress that was knee-length on me, but almost a floor-length gown on her. She had draped multiple rhinestone necklaces around her neck and bracelets up her bare arms.

"I'm your host of today's show, Hailey!" Hailey announced. "Zillions of dancers tried out, but only five remain. Today we find out which of the finalists will be crowned Hailey's Best Dancer!"

"Is this like the TV show?" Lily asked me.

"Kind of." I nodded and grinned.

I looked at the other girls, hoping they would think this was fun and not dumb. I knew Hailey being cute would help them play along, and I was right.

"This is going to be fun!" Megan said.

"Yeah!" Riley added.

"Come in, contestants!" Hailey flung open the door of her room. Hailey's room was the same size as mine, but while I had wanted more floor space, she had wanted a big bed.

"Your bedroom is cute," Trina said.

"Bedroom?" Hailey sniffed into the mic. "This is the Hailey TV Studios, and you're live! Each of you will be given a dance to perform, and the top two will go into the finals and win a quarter of a billion dollars! Who will walk away with the title of Hailey's Best Dancer?"

We all played along and yelled: "ME!" Hailey had us stand up along her wall.

Hailey explained the rules of the game, which we had

played together lots of times in Connecticut. Every "contestant" would have to perform a dance chosen randomly. We would choose an "all-star dance partner"—but it would have to be an inanimate object. Her bed would be the stage.

"You'll be judged by our three esteemed judges." Hailey pointed to her fluffy white circle chair and we all started cracking up. Lined up were a teddy bear, a robotic dog, and a small doll modeled after a famous dancer.

Hailey had us sit, held out her cupped hands, and made us each pick a piece of paper. Mine said number two: ballet.

"Our first contestant is . . ." Hailey waited, but nobody responded. "Hello? Whose paper says number one?"

"Oh, me!" Trina waved her paper. "It says number one: lyrical."

"Introducing Trina with a lyrical piece!" Hailey announced. "Please get your celebrity partner and go onstage. No live people."

Trina looked around.

"Hurry! Grab something. We're live!" Hailey yelled at her. Trina went over and grabbed Hailey's hairbrush. We all started laughing.

"What's your theme?" Lily called out. "We should have a theme."

"Good idea." Hailey nodded.

"Okay, my theme is sadness and pain." Trina held up her prop. "Specifically, the pain of getting my hair done for a competition."

We all started laughing so hard. Something we could all relate to.

"Preach!" Lily yelled.

Hailey started the music, a slow song with a woman singing sadly.

Trina jumped on the bed and danced with the brush. She waved it gently in the air, then dropped down and rolled on the bed. Then she reached out toward us, brushed her hair up into a bun, making pained faces, and held it with her hand. Finally, she whirled around, holding her head as if in pain, and posed dramatically.

"Wooo!" we all cheered.

"That was our first contestant, Trina. So authentic, so relatable," Hailey said into the mic.

"You should consider this for a career," Lily told Hailey.

"No trying to sway the judge with compliments!" Megan barked. "Even if she is the cutest thing!"

"That's a compliment too!" Lily shot back, laughing.

"No, no, don't stop the compliments," Hailey encouraged. "Keep them coming."

"Hey! You can't mess with the judging process," I protested.

"But she's not even the judge," Trina said, looking confused. "They're the judges."

We all looked at the teddy bear, robot, and doll. And we all started laughing.

"Um . . . Trina," Megan started to say.

"See! So, don't waste your time complimenting my annoying little sister," I said, waving my piece of paper in the air. "Let's get on with the show."

"Hey!" Hailey said. "Oh, look who our next contestant is. The annoying *big* sister, Harper."

"Ooooh," Megan said. "Don't insult the host! You've been insulted in front of a worldwide audience."

She high-fived my sister.

"Ouch!" I laughed. "I hadn't thought that through!"

It was my turn. I hadn't really thought this through either. I looked around for my prop.

"I have a ballet dance." I jumped on the bed. "Which, FYI, speaking from previous experience, is hard to do on Hailey's bed because it's so bouncy."

"No excuses in dance competitions," Hailey scolded. "Although, yes, I do have a soft, bouncy bed. Too bad, so sad."

Hailey turned on ballet music and I posed on top of the bed like a ballerina.

"Wait, where's your partner?" Lily asked.

"You'll see," I said.

When the music started, I melted on top of the bed, sliding over so my head was nearly on the floor. From this position, I could see under Hailey's bed. As I also knew from previous experience, it was a disaster. And her hiding place for snacks. I grabbed a box of cheese crackers and pulled it out from underneath.

And I began dancing with it like a partner.

Everyone cracked up.

"She's dancing with cheese crackers." Trina was doubled over, laughing.

I was. I danced what I would say was a beautiful—okay, maybe not beautiful, but interesting—interpretive ballet dance with my box of crackers. I did an impressive arabesque and a not-as-impressive leap from one end of the bed to the other. I saved my favorite move for the grand finale as I lay back on the bed, my head dangling down as I flowed my hands to put the cracker box back under the bed. Then I did a back walkover to the floor. Not a ballet move, but one I thought looked cool.

When the song was over, everyone applauded and I bowed.

"Oh wait, I forgot to say my theme is snacks," I said. "I mean, who doesn't love a good snack?"

"Uh," Hailey said. "You're not going to tell Mom about my snack stash, are you?"

"Depends if you vote for me to win." I smiled.

"RIGGED!" everyone started yelling. "RIGGED!"

"Okay, okay! I take it back!" I laughed. "I promise I won't tell."

Hailey went right back into her emcee mode.

"That was our second contestant, Harper, with a lovely, although cheesy, ballet number," Hailey said. "Clean lines and good technique, but your partner was a bit stiff."

"Wow, you really know how to critique," Lily said.

"She watches a lot of dance shows with me," I said.

"The dance was also a little boring," Hailey added.

"Hey!" I said. "You didn't insult the other dancer!"

"Ha! I thought since you're her sister you'd automatically win." Riley snickered.

"Nope." Hailey smiled smugly. "Why would I vote for my annoying sister?"

"You're annoying," I shot back.

"My little sister is annoying too," Riley said to me.

"Thank you." I bumped fists with Riley in solidarity.

"Our next contestant is Riley!" Hailey announced after Riley raised her hand. "Who has an automatic deduction for insulting little sisters."

"Augh!" Riley said. "I take it back! Little sisters are the best!"

We all cheered for Riley.

"I'm doing a jazz number," Riley said. "With my partner, Pool Noodle. My theme is ninja dancer."

She picked up Hailey's pool noodle and jumped on the bed. Hailey started the music and Riley danced. She twirled and swished the pool noodle around and up in the air as she did a jump. As the music got more dramatic, she used it like a sword over her head, slashing through the air. For her final move, she jabbed the sword at the judges and at us, then jumped off the bed using the noodle as a jump rope.

We all applauded and cheered.

"Powerful moves and impressive partner usage from our contestant, Riley! Let's see what the judges think so far." Hailey went up to the immobile judges. "They aren't giving anything away. Our fourth contestant is—"

Hailey was interrupted by scratching at the door.

"Mo wants to come in." I smiled and opened the door. Mo raced in carrying his rubber chew toy, sniffed at each of the girls, and then jumped up on the fluffy white chair, knocking the robot dog off in the process.

"Mo wants to be a judge!" Trina said. "He's taking over for Robot Dog."

Mo sat on the chair and chewed his toy.

"Remember who feeds you treats, Judge Mo," I said to him.

"No swaying the judges!" Lily swatted me. Then she jumped up and picked up Robot Dog. "And I now have my partner for my hip-hop routine. My theme is robots."

She jumped up on the bed and placed the robot dog next to her. Hailey turned on the hip-hop music, which jammed loudly through the room.

Lily turned on the robotic dog, who beeped and lit up. As the dog moved its head side to side, Lily did too.

We all started cracking up as Lily did robot moves next to it. She made some precise movements along with the robot, popping and locking.

Everyone was laughing hysterically.

Lily shifted into high-energy hip-hop moves for her dance. She held up Robot Dog and did a strong heel stretch. Then when she put Robot Dog down for her final spin on the bed, he dramatically bounced off onto the rug and under the bed.

"Oh, no! My partner!" Lily gasped.

I dove off Hailey's bed and found Robot Dog where he had wedged himself among all of the serious mess underneath.

"Is he okay?"

"I can't tell!" I wedged myself in farther. "He's not lighting up. . . ."

"Noooo! Robot Dog, don't die!" I could hear Hailey's dramatic voice from above. "You have so much to live for!"

"Wait, he's really alive?" Trina asked. "I thought it was a toy."

I finally got a grip on the robot and scooted myself backward with him in my hand. I pressed his ears—and he lit up and made noises.

"He's fine," I said, panting. "I'm not sure about me. Hailey, you have to clean out underneath your bed. I almost suffocated."

"Well, what's most important is that Robot Dog is okay," Hailey said, cradling the robot dog, who bleeped at her.

"You're welcome for the rescue," I said to her and shook my head. Then I heard crying sounds behind me.

Lily was fake-sobbing.

"Was I that bad that my partner leapt to his doom to escape?" Lily asked.

"No, you were amazing—for ratings! Now, that's the kind of scandal that brings TV viewers!" Hailey said. Then she grabbed her microphone. "The only way to describe it is you have swag, Lily."

Lily bowed.

We all cheered. Mo barked along, sharing the excitement.

Hailey placed the robot dog on her dresser and Mo back on the judges' chair.

"Our final contestant is . . . Megan!" she announced.

"Thank you, thank you. I'll be performing a contemporary dance with my partner . . ." She went over and picked up Mo.

"Cheating! Cheating!" we all yelled. "You can't have the judge as a partner."

"But he's sooo cute," Megan said, putting him back down on the chair. "Please, Hailey?"

"What do you think, Mo?" Hailey said and held Mo out toward Megan. Megan leaned in and made kissy faces. And, of course, Mo kissed her.

"That's a yes!" Megan said, and took Mo on the bed with her. "My theme is cute puppies!"

We all groaned. Megan was obviously a master manipulator.

"Be careful," Riley cautioned. Megan rolled her eyes.

The music started, and Megan did a gentle contemporary dance with Mo, who was happy when cradled in her arms. She danced beautifully, then put him down and did a needle with her hands on the bed next to him and her leg in the air. Mo started to bark up at her and race around on the bed in circles. Megan picked him up and posed with him to end her dance.

We all applauded for her as she and Mo hopped off the bed.

"Wow!" Hailey spoke into her mic. "Let's give a round of applause to all of our contestants! And now let's see what our judges think."

She moved the microphone to the doll and the teddy bear and then chased a lively Mo around the room.

"The judges have weighed in," Hailey said. "It's a hard decision. It's hard judging people."

Actually, I realized it was kind of easy to judge people. I looked at the Bunheads. I'd been judging them this whole time. They were actually pretty fun. As long as they weren't being mean, we might be able to all get along. I smiled.

"In last place is Harper, because her dance was boring." Hailey knocked me out of my thoughts.

"Last place?" The smiled dropped off my face. "I demand a recount! I lost to someone who almost killed your robot dog?"

"You know I'm not a fan of ballet." Hailey shrugged. "Please show good sportsmanship."

I threw a pillow at her. She laughed and ducked. I laughed too.

"In fourth place for her lyrical dance is Trina!"

"Woo hoo!" Trina danced around excitedly.

"Fourth place out of five," Megan said to her.

"I know!" Trina continued her happy dance.

"And in third place is Riley!" Hailey pointed to Riley,

and we all clapped for her as she slashed her ninja pool noodle around.

"And the moment we've been waiting for . . . ," Hailey said. Then she deepened her voice. "Is your phone ready for an upgrade?"

Everyone groaned.

"No commercials, Hailey," I said.

"Okay, okay," Hailey said. "Our runner-up is . . . Lily!"

"I WON!" Megan seemed genuinely excited as Hailey went and got one of her princess crowns and placed it on Megan's head. "I won!"

"Of course you won—you danced with a dog!" Riley said. "Who can compete with a cute puppy?"

"Shout-out to Mo!" Megan blew him a kiss.

I grinned. We were all cracking up.

"And did Lily get second because she also danced with a dog?" I asked. "Even though she tried to break him?"

"He jumped! Which is maybe worse," Lily said. Then she turned to Megan and gave her a high five. "Dogs for the win!"

"Take it up with the judges," Hailey told me.

I went to the judges' seat, picked up the teddy bear, and tossed it at Hailey.

"My partner's feelings are hurt," I said. I picked up one of the pillows and threw it at Hailey. She grabbed another one and threw it back.

"Pillow fight!" Trina yelled.

Everyone grabbed a pillow—and Riley had her pool noodle—and we all started hitting each other. I stood for a second and looked at everyone having fun. This was what I'd been hoping for. Then I hit each of the Bunheads with a pillow.

I had just gotten bopped by Lily and fallen over onto the bed when the door opened.

"Sna . . . ACK!" My mom poked her head in the door.

Megan's pillow flew at my mom's head, and she ducked just in time!

"Sorry! Sorry, sorry!" Megan said.

"I'll try that again." My mom smiled. "Snacks in the kitchen if you'd like to—"

Yes! Everyone dropped their pillows and raced out the door. My mom waited until everyone had headed out into the hallway before she whispered to me.

"Are you having fun with your team?" She didn't whisper quietly enough.

"YES!" Riley turned around and said.

Yay.

After yesterday, I felt much better about our team spirit. I went into our rehearsal feeling good about things. We were all much nicer on the way in. And excited.

Dress rehearsal! We put on our costumes for the first time and went into the studio.

"We look awesome!" Riley said.

We did. Vanessa had wanted our first costumes to reflect our studio colors. Our leotards were white with beautiful silver rhinestones. A flowing skirt made of light ribbons of fabric in pink and white swirled around my legs as I twirled. It was one of the prettiest costumes I had ever had.

We all swirled and twirled as the ribbons fluttered around us.

But things quickly got serious when Vanessa came in.

"This is our final run-through," she said. "Let's knock this out."

She had us run through the routine. And then run through it again. And again.

Vanessa was in beast mode.

"Watch your step," Megan snapped at Riley. "Watch your arms." At Lily. "Watch your face." At Trina.

If Vanessa was in beast mode, Megan was really wound up.

When rehearsal was over, Vanessa stood in front of us.

"That was an okay rehearsal," she said. "Okay, but not great."

"You know the saying: A bad dress rehearsal means a good performance!" Trina said.

"There is also a saying that practice makes perfect," Vanessa said. "And that was far from perfect. Stretch tonight! See you tomorrow."

Everything was super tense. As we walked out, I tried to end on an uplifting note.

"Guys, remember last night," I said on the way out. "We were all getting along! Let's be a team!"

"A team that forgets their routine," Megan said, giving Riley a side eye.

"It was one time!" Riley protested. "If you'd stop glaring at me, I might remember it."

Later that night in bed, I couldn't sleep. I was tossing and turning, thinking about the competition. It was tomorrow! My first competition with my new studio! It was really happening!

Then I got a text from Lily.

don't worry about it!!! 😉

I smiled.

how did u know I was up worrying?! 🙂 im ok

Lily texted back.

i'm glad you're not too upset! don't let them get to u!

Huh?

don't let who get to me?

I waited a few moments. I could see Lily was typing, but then it kept stopping. I texted again.

WHAT

Lily texted me.

nothing! that wasn't for u! go to sleep!

I could tell it wasn't nothing. What was it? A group text I wasn't included in? A social media post? I scrolled through social media. And then I saw it.

The video. I hadn't seen it at first, but Megan was tagged on it.

There I was. First you saw me smiling happily and dancing on the parade float. Then you saw me jump, hit Trina, and fall toward the edge of the float. The camera zoomed close up on me as my face twisted in horror and—

I fell in SLOW MOTION.

Slo-mo me was making a really ridiculous face and falling, falling toward the camera. Ugh, Hailey had been right that my arms did flail on the way down. I had to give myself props, though, on my landing, which was on my knees, versus other, more embarrassing places.

Then I threw up my hands, like I was a gymnast sticking a landing or something. Oh, I was totally embarrassing.

And it was now on social media for everyone to see, up close.

I looked to see who had posted it. It was anonymous, but it had already gotten forty-two likes. I knew who it had to be. It had to be the Bells. If they were trying to shake me up, they were doing a good job. My hands were shaking when I texted Lily back.

o no. did the bunheads see it?

There was a pause.

i don't know. It's pretty late. maybe they're sleeping. hey! It's 11:11! MAKE A WISH!

My door suddenly opened and my mom stuck her head in.

"Harper! Are you on your phone? You need to get your sleep!" she said.

"But—"

"No buts," she said. "Hand over your phone. You have a big day tomorrow."

Reluctantly, I handed her my phone. It was probably for the best. I didn't really want to know anything else. If the Bunheads and everyone at DanceStarz hadn't already seen it, they certainly would before the competition.

I lay in my bed, blinking back tears. But I did make a wish. And finally, finally I fell asleep.

efore a competition is always chaos. Younger kids go earlier in the day, when things are quieter, but by the time I walked in with my mom, it was chaos. Other dance companies were arriving like us, with their giant duffel bags taking up half the hallways. Or they were running through the halls to get to the stage to compete.

"Where is registration . . . ?" My mom looked around. "Oh! There's your team. Go on. I'll see you in a minute."

I saw the Bunheads together, wearing the same team jacket and warm-up pants that I had on. I dreaded facing them.

"Hi," I mumbled.

"Harper!" Megan said. "You're here. Where's Lily?"

"She's on her way," I said. "She just texted me. Look. About that video—"

"We are *not* going to talk about that video," Megan said through clenched teeth. "We are not going to *think* about that video. They wanted to shake us up. We will *not* let them."

"Sounds good to me," I said. But Megan was obviously shaken. I looked at Riley and Trina, and they both looked away.

Lily ran up to us.

"How are you?" she asked me.

"Not thinking about that video," I whispered back.

Vanessa came up to us.

"You have a few hours until call time," Vanessa told us. "I'm going to go look at the stage setup, and I'll find you in the dressing room."

"Let's try to get a small room," Megan said. Sometimes you can find an empty smaller room to get ready and zone out in peace. We looked into two rooms that were full and then into a third one that was really full: of Energii.

It seemed like every single one of them looked at us and smirked.

"This room is *taken*," one of them called out. None of us wanted to deal with that now. We backed away. But we were too late.

"Don't fall off the stage!" one of them yelled.

"Isabelle," Megan whispered. She looked at me. My face flamed red.

"That is so not cool," Lily said.

"We are *not* going to let them affect us," Megan repeated.

I twirled my hair and tried not to let them get to me. We went to the big room backstage where most of the teams were preparing.

"Grab a corner!" Megan hissed to us, and we all looked around wildly for some space to claim for our team. People were racing around in costume or in half of their costumes looking for the rest of their group or looking for their mothers to do their hair. Some people were practicing their moves. When a coach called to her team to go to the stage, we quickly moved in and took over their space.

We had a lot to do.

The moms came in with the competition stuff: the booklet to show who was performing when. Riley took it and flipped through it quickly.

"Small group juniors category." Riley showed us in the booklet. "DanceStarz Squad! There we are!"

"And there's Energii." Megan frowned, pointing at their

names. "They're in small group juniors too. Doing a lyrical routine."

I put my stuff down on the floor next to the mirror. The moms, plus Trina's sister, got to work doing our hair. We had to have our headpieces pinned in. The headpieces were white lace with gold and pink jewels sewn in. They were super pretty and somewhat painful to put on. My mom crisscrossed bobby pins to hold it tight to my head and in front of my bun.

"Ow." I winced.

"Sorry," my mom said.

"I know," I told her. I knew she had to do it. Once, my headpiece had flown off. I'd kept dancing, but I'd had to keep making sure I didn't slip on it. Plus, as I later saw on the competition video, my hair was then sticking up ridiculously.

So I let Mom stab at me with bobby pins. When she finished, I admired her work in the mirror. "It looks great, Mom. No wispies."

She leaned down to give me a hug. I expected her to say something warm and fuzzy about not worrying because it was my first time.

"This is your first time with DanceStarz," she said. "We want to show them what you can do. You need to prove yourself."

I was a little surprised at how fierce she sounded. But I knew she only wanted me to do my best, because she knew that I'd be happy about it later. I was a perfectionist at competitions, and afterward I got really picky about my dancing and dwelled on my mistakes. The best way to avoid this was to nail it.

"Okay." I nodded. *Dancer beast mode, on.*

My mom sprayed me with about half a can of hairspray. Then she got a text.

"I'm going to go grab good seats. Break a leg," she said.

A group came in wearing large costumes. And by "large," I mean really large because they were dressed as giraffes. Their giraffe heads bobbed on long necks a foot higher than their real heads.

"That's . . . creative," Lily mumbled to me.

"That stunk," one of the giraffes grumbled.

"I never, ever want to dance in a giant giraffe head again," another one said.

That sounded reasonable to me.

It was time to do makeup. We all sat cross-legged in front of a dressing mirror. I put on my makeup carefully, making sure it was intense enough to be seen out in the audience.

"Sunshine Dance Studio, five minutes!" somebody called out.

The dance team next to me all shrieked a little and started rehearsing their dance aggressively. So aggressively one of them kicked super close to my head!

"Excuse me!" I said.

"Sorry." The girl smiled apologetically.

I did not want to be kicked in the head right before my dance. I had enough problems: nerves. Stomach butterflies. Megan. The Bells. My first time dancing onstage in Florida.

Deep breath. I had to think positive. I was going to only surround myself with positivity.

"Oops!" Someone tripped over my foot. I pulled back, thinking it was an accident, until I saw the look on Trina's face.

It was Bella, with Isabelle.

"Don't you have your own room?" Lily asked them.

"We just came out to wish you good luck," Isabelle said. "I know that's bad luck, but if I said break a leg I'm afraid that one would take it literally and fall off the stage."

I stood up.

"I know you posted that video," I said.

The Bells cracked up.

"Could have been anyone." Isabelle shrugged, grinning. "There were hundreds of people there watching that humiliating dance of your so-called Squad."

"Go back to your new team," Megan said. "Traitors."

"I'm a traitor? You're the traitor," Isabelle said.

"How am I the traitor?" Megan asked. "You ditched us for Energii!"

"Well what did you expect us to do?" Isabelle challenged her, hand on her hip.

"Be on the Squad?" Megan replied.

"Yeah, ha-ha," Bella said. "After Vanessa told us we might not be a 'fit'?"

Oh. OH. That explained a lot.

"It's not like you even cared," Isabelle continued.

"Wait, what?" Megan jumped up and faced Isabelle. "I didn't even know."

"Nice try," Isabelle said. "And then you were all like, Yay me! Go Squad!"

"I thought you were going to be on the Squad! How was I supposed to know you weren't?" Megan half wailed.

"From when we texted you?" Isabelle said. "Helloooo? Earth to Megan?"

"You never texted me!" Megan shook her head.

"Don't act all innocent! We signed up for Energii right away, and texted you to come, and you texted back no way, you were not coming with us!"

"What are you talking about? I never texted that!" Megan said.

The two of them were so locked in eye contact, they didn't even notice Bella was slowly inching backward.

"Bella texted you. I told Bella to text you," Isabelle said slowly.

Everyone turned toward Bella.

"Oh," Bella said. "Huh. Maybe the text didn't go through!"

"But you said she answered," Isabelle said, "that she said no way would she come with us."

"Uh," Bella said. "Heh. Uh. Well! I just thought because she didn't answer, she didn't want to come with us. By not answering, that's an answer! Yeah."

"You never texted me, did you?" Megan went up to Bella's face.

"I think I did?" Bella said.

"You didn't want me to come with you!" Megan accused.

"Um," Bella said, and looked around wildly. "Gotta go."

Bella scurried away. Isabelle turned to leave too.

"Isabelle! Wait! See? It wasn't my fault," Megan said frantically. "None of this is my fault! You can't be mad at me!"

Megan's voice was rising. People from the other studios were turning to look at us.

"It was a misunderstanding!" Megan said. "We can go back to the way it was!"

The girls around us started giggling.

"Fight!" one of the giraffes called out.

"Megan, you're causing a scene," Isabelle said calmly. "You know I hate any drama before I dance. It takes me out of my zone."

"But you started the drama!" I jumped in.

"Isabelle!" Megan said softly.

Isabelle softened for a minute.

"Megan. It's my first competition with Energii," she said. "Okay? It's done. They're my team now. We need to focus on the competition."

She turned around and left. We all stood in silence, watching her.

"Um." I tried to break the awkward silence. "Whew. That was a lot."

Megan stood there looking furious. Then she looked at us looking at her.

"What?" she snapped. "You heard her. Focus on the competition. Get in the zone. Let's stretch!"

I cringed but followed her lead as we dropped down on the floor to stretch. Megan stuck her legs out forward, pulled on her feet, and laid her face down on her knees. We all followed her, although there wasn't much room as other dance teams came in and squashed the area.

"Well, I'm glad that's over!" Riley said with an awkward little laugh.

Megan whipped her head up.

"Do you even understand what just happened? Bella sabotaged me!" Megan spat.

"I get it." Riley leaned back. "I just meant—"

"Bella never sent the text. She didn't want me to know they were going to Energii!" Megan continued. "She was jealous of me because I was becoming a better dancer than she was! She thought I would take her place in the Bells and be Isabelle's best friend!"

Maybe that was true.

"Or maybe she just doesn't like you," Riley said.

Trina gasped.

"I mean, I don't know!" Riley backtracked. "Just saying. But what difference does it really make? You wouldn't have gone with them anyway."

Megan opened her mouth—and shut it again.

"You wouldn't have gone with them, would you have? I mean, we'd already made the Squad. The Bunheads *made* the

Squad." Riley's eyes narrowed as Megan didn't respond. "You would have gone with the Bells?"

"I didn't say that!" Megan rolled her eyes.

"But you didn't NOT say that!" Riley said. "Did you want to go with them? Did you want to take Bella's place in the Bells and be Isabelle's best friend?! Instead of *mine*? She was right! You would have ditched us!"

"I-I didn't say that!" Megan stammered. "I didn't—I mean I don't even! I'm going to the bathroom!"

Megan jumped up. Just as a team of dancers passed by after their musical theater routine. Megan knocked into one of them, who stumbled back—and stepped down with her high heels . . .

Right on Riley's hand.

"Why did it have to be a character shoe?" Lily moaned. "That heel must have really hurt!"

"I know," I said miserably.

Riley had let out a scream that stopped everything in the entire room. Her mother had raced over and whisked her out the door, and Vanessa had followed them. We'd been sitting on the floor ever since.

"It wasn't my fault," Megan said.

Nobody responded. We halfheartedly stretched in silence.

Then Vanessa came back in the room. She came over to us.

"The good news is Riley's hand will be okay. It's bruised and painful," she said. "But she's cleared to dance."

We all exhaled with relief.

"Riley assured me it was an accident." Vanessa paused. "But sometimes carelessness is an issue. So it might be best to pull the number."

"NO!" Megan and I both shouted.

"It's our first chance to perform," Megan said. "We really want to dance."

"I don't know," Vanessa hedged. "Riley cannot put pressure on her hand. And that's part of the choreography. The other option is we run the number without Riley."

I thought about what Vanessa had told me. *Speak up! Step up to the plate.*

"Vanessa, we only want to dance as a team," I said. "We should only dance if you'll let Riley do it."

"Well—"

"We'll rechoreograph it!" I continued. "Trina can teach it to her quickly. You know Trina is a good teacher."

"Well," Vanessa said. "That would mean taking out Riley's hand-walking, and we have to replace Riley and Megan's partner trick. Hm. Lily may be able to fill in for the hand-walking."

Lily made a panicky face. I knew she could do it, though. She was athletic and even stronger than ever.

"What is most problematic is the partner trick," Vanessa continued. "It's a highlight of the dance."

That was the challenge. Megan and Riley's partnering section was one of the most impressive, showiest parts of the dance and would get us points for performance and difficulty. I knew we needed something that would be as, if not more, showstopping.

And I had an idea. I thought back to that first class we'd taken, when I'd had to do the lyrical freestyle competition. The one where Megan had rolled under me and I had spun and kicked right over her. The one that had made everyone gasp and resulted in my winning the freestyle competition.

I quickly explained what I was thinking.

"You know, that could work," Vanessa said, nodding. "I'm not saying yes. But I'm not saying no. Let me go see when Riley's hand will be bandaged and ask her mother."

She left.

"Okay! So it looks like—"

"I have to go to the girls' room!" Megan said. She fled.

"Do you think we should help her?" I asked.

"Help her go to the bathroom?" Trina asked.

"I think it was more than that," I said. "I think we should go check on her."

We all went down the hallway to the bathroom. When we got there, a girl was running out, looking terrified.

"I wouldn't go in there," the girl warned. "This girl in there? Hissed at me. Really scary."

"Uh-oh. Megan." Trina shook her head. "I'm not going in there."

"I will." I sighed. I pushed the door open. "Um. Megan? It's me."

Megan groaned from inside a stall. "Just leave!"

"Look. I'm not leaving until you tell me what's going on."

"Didn't you hear Vanessa?" Megan spat. "She knows. She knows I caused it."

"Megan, she said she thinks it was an accident. It really was an accident," I said. "We all know it."

"You all know that if Riley and I hadn't been fighting, it wouldn't have happened," Megan said. "It's like everything is going wrong on this team."

"We know," I said. "Riley is okay. We all will be okay—if you get up and dance."

"We're losing two of our most impressive moves," Megan said. "Our routine will be weak. Vanessa's probably right. We shouldn't perform. We're just going to humiliate ourselves in front of . . . everybody."

At that moment, the door of the girls' room flew open.

"By 'everybody,' you mean the Bells." Trina had come in. "That's all you care about. Seriously, if you want to go join Energii, just go already. They're right down the hall; go join them."

"It's not that . . . ," Megan said, almost crying. "Well, maybe that's a little true. I don't want to go with the Bells. I want to stay with this school! We've been here forever. And I want to stay with the Bunheads!"

I felt bad.

"And you want to stay with the Bells, too," I said. Then I realized something. "You're actually a loyal person, aren't you? You wanted everyone together. Look, I know you feel abandoned. But we're still here for you."

"I just wish . . . I wish everything could be the way it was," Megan said softly.

"I know what you mean." I leaned against a sink. "Change is . . . weird. I left my team and my friends, and I have to start all over on this team. I have to be honest, it's not going so great so far."

"I knew it! You're ditching us! You're going to join Energii too, aren't you, Harper?" Trina moaned.

"What? No!" I said. That thought hadn't even crossed my

mind! Well, since after the parade, when I confirmed their auditions were completely closed. "You know what? There's only one reason I will ditch. And that's if we give up. What's the point of being on a competition dance team if we don't compete—or dance?"

The door to the bathroom stall swung open. Megan came out. Her eyes were red, but she wasn't crying.

"That actually is a good point," she said. "I do *not* give up. We'll dance. We'll compete."

"Yay!" Trina clapped her hands.

"Well, if Riley will dance," I added. "She was pretty upset. And her whole hand and everything."

"I'll just tell Riley she has to dance," Megan said fiercely.

"I don't know that Riley is going to take your orders just like that anymore." Trina crossed her arms. *Yowch.* Looked like Trina wasn't going to take it anymore either.

"I'll *ask* Riley to dance," Megan amended. Trina nodded.

"Let's go find Riley," I said. "Lily! We're coming out. Move away from the door!"

I waited and pushed open the door. Lily stepped back away from it. Megan and Trina went out ahead of me, and Megan put her arm around Trina affectionately.

"How did you know I was eavesdropping?" Lily waited

for me. We followed the other two down the hallway.

"I could see your eyeball," I joked. "You could have come in. You're part of the team. I wanted you to hear that, anyway."

"No way. I was terrified." Lily laughed. Then she got serious. "I hope we can dance. The only thing more humiliating than dancing badly is to not be allowed to dance at all."

"Lily's right." Megan turned around. "Let's make this happen."

Lily and I grinned at each other.

We went back to the changing room. And Riley was there!

"Riley!" We all rushed at her. Megan and Trina went to hug her.

"Careful of the hand!" her mother cautioned us. Riley held up a hand wrapped in a bulky tan bandage wrap.

"You know that was an accident," Megan said. "And I'm sorry. About everything."

"Oh," Riley said. "Oh, good! That's good."

"May I hug you too?" Lily asked her. Riley nodded. *Aw.* I joined them in a big group hug.

"Team hug!" Trina squealed. "I am so emotional right now!"

"Gross. Hugs," a voice said behind me.

I broke free to see my sister standing behind me. Riley's sister was next to her.

"Stop the hugfest and let's focus on the real issue," Hailey said. She held up a pair of scissors.

And before I realized what she was doing, she cut off one of my ribbons. Everyone gasped.

"HAILEY!" My jaw dropped. "What are you doing?!"

"We had a brilliant idea," Hailey said. "Don't worry, Vanessa told us we should do it. Trina, don't move."

She clipped off one of Trina's side ribbons as Riley's sister, Quinn, explained.

"Riley, we know how much you love your costumes," she said. "So we want to cover up that ugly hand thing. You can wrap the ribbons around your hand and it will match!"

That was so sweet! Riley looked touched. She hugged her sister. Then she hugged mine: a huge, smothering hug. Hailey's face looked desperate.

"Your sister's being squashed," Lily whispered to me.

"Hailey's not a big hugger," I said to her, and we both cracked up when Hailey poked her head under Riley's arm and mouthed to me: *Help!*

"Riley," I said. "We should get ready."

"Okay," she said, letting a relieved Hailey go. Hailey grabbed Quinn's wrist and they raced out of the room.

We all helped Riley prop up her arm and wrap the ribbons

around her hand. Megan took over at the end and tied the ribbons together around her wrist with an adorable bow.

"This actually looks cute," Riley said.

"Maybe you can add it to your fashion line," Lily said. "Dance gloves by Riley."

"Super cute," Megan said.

"Now we just need Vanessa to tell us we can dance."

"But I can't do all the moves," Riley said, worried.

"Here's the plan," I said. I told them how Vanessa had suggested Lily do the hand-walking instead. Lily apologized to Riley for taking her trick, but Riley looked relieved. And then I told them my other idea. "Instead of Riley and Megan's partner trick, Riley, you'll join the trio and Megan and I will do our partner trick."

As I explained, I could tell Riley felt a little sad.

"As soon as you're better, you can do your partner trick with Megan," I reassured her.

"Thanks." Riley seemed to appreciate it. "Actually, this is kind of good. It's something the Bells haven't seen before, unlike Megan's and my trick, which Isabelle actually taught us in the first place."

"Oh!" Megan said. "That is true."

"And it's something they can't do—because the Bells can't

pirouette nearly as well as Harper," Riley said. "So that's a good idea."

Lily caught my eye and smiled at me.

"Let's walk it through. If we can do this, Vanessa will have to let us dance," Megan said. She got up, took a deep breath—and went back into queen-bee mode. She went to a corner of the room where some dancers were sitting and waiting. I don't know what she said, but they jumped up and moved and she had commandeered a space for us to do a run-through. She started giving us orders.

We walked through the dance. Where Riley and Megan's partner section originally had been, Riley was now going to take my part and move to the back. Lily, Riley, and Trina would pose off to the sides, and Megan and I would move to the front of the stage.

I would be doing my turn series. Megan would do a high jump and then slide right toward me. At the last minute, she would go right into an arch, and I would straighten my leg as I turned to kick right over her.

It was going to be tricky to get the timing right.

"You do know if you miss the timing, you'll kick me in the face," Megan said.

"Yeah," I said. "So it's a win-win."

It took everyone a second. Then I started laughing.

"I'm *joking*!" I said.

"You better be," Megan said, but she was grinning too.

I was happy to lighten the mood for a second. Because soon, it was going to get intense. Just this partnering trick alone was a challenge.

If it worked, it was going to be really impressive. But if it didn't . . . I shuddered. I didn't want to think about that. We ran through it a couple times. There wasn't enough space to actually do it, but we talked through our timing the best we could.

And when Vanessa came in, she looked at us and we knew she agreed with our decision.

We were going to dance.

ALL TIME!

There would be two more dances and then—we'd be on. We waited silently off in the wings.

Energii was onstage now, but Megan had instructed us to face the other way so we couldn't sneak peeks. She didn't want us to be intimidated by their dance. After they were done, the crowd cheered super loud.

Uh, yeah, that was intimidating.

Then Energii came running out, excited, right past us. Isabelle stopped near Megan and opened her mouth to say something.

"DON'T EVEN."

To everyone's surprise, that was Trina. Trina had gotten right in Isabelle's face.

Isabelle obviously was surprised too. She stepped back and smirked, but then continued on without saying anything.

"Nice," Megan whispered to Trina. "Let's huddle."

We huddled in a circle.

"Okay," Megan said. "Remember the corrections Vanessa gave us."

I thought about my most recent corrections: Don't tense up my face. Really stretch through my feet.

"Remember to connect with the audience," Trina whispered.

"And watch your feet," I whispered.

"Be high energy," Riley whispered.

"And powerful," Lily said.

"Okay! It's our first time dancing together at a competition," Trina said. "That's really special. We've learned to work together as a team. . . ."

She paused and looked at Riley's hand.

"We're *learning* to work together as a team." Trina changed it. "We're here to represent Vanessa and DanceStarz Squad. Let's be thankful for this opportunity to dance! Let's tell our story in our dance."

And we all did our new ritual.

We'd made it up as a team. No Bells, no Bunheads, and definitely no plugging your nose and making swim movements. Hee.

We whispered:

"Dance!"

And did a little dance.

"Starz!"

We fluttered our fingers like sparkling stars.

Then we leaned into a huddle and whispered:

"Squad!"

I stepped back. I wanted to have a few seconds for myself, to get into my zone. I closed my eyes. I could feel my heartbeat, my adrenaline racing. I closed my eyes and tried to picture myself dancing perfectly. I would hold my head high. I would point my toes! I'd loosen up my face and stretch through my feet! I'd be perfect with my leap! My turns! My . . . my . . . my . . . my . . .

And suddenly, I couldn't remember my dance.

I couldn't remember my dance! I couldn't remember my dance!

The dancers who were on before us came running off the stage. It was our turn! We were up next and I couldn't remember my dance!

"I can't remember my dance!" I whispered.

Of all people, Megan looked at me.

"Me neither," she said. Then she looked hard at me. "We'll be fine."

The announcer's voice boomed through the backstage.

"Please welcome to the stage, DanceStarz with the contemporary routine: 'Awaken'!"

I felt my adrenaline practically burst through my body, and I walked onstage in a line with my team.

I took my place in the formation. My heart was pounding. I took a deep breath. And the music began.

And I danced.

Most of it was a blur. I didn't pay any attention to the audience, or the judges in front of me making notes, or anything except my teammates and the dance. I just let my body feel the music and do the steps we'd be rehearsing, letting my muscle memory take over. But just before we got to the part we changed today, I jumped into focus. This was it.

As we planned, Riley took a few steps back. I went up to center stage to prep for my turn series.

At first, it was a normal turn series. I did a pirouette and then another. Then I did a kick spin. This was where we had to get the timing PERFECT.

Megan did a leap toward me. Just like in our lyrical improv, it looked like she was going to crash into me. I actually heard the audience gasp. Then Megan slid forward on the ground so that she was right underneath my leg. Just as my leg would have hit her, she melted down into a hinge.

I twirled with my leg horizontal over her—and then she popped up. Then I twirled back over her, and she ducked down, over and over again. I finished with a turn holding my leg high and straight, with Megan underneath me, and held it for a few seconds.

We did it!

I grinned and then moved to the next combination 500 percent full-out. We were really connecting as a group and I felt our energy. I did the jumps and the poses and the moves.

This was why I danced! I felt like I was showing my passion for the audience, for the judges, and for myself. I was in the zone!

Then the music ended. I dropped to the floor and held my final pose.

And we were done!

I was breathing hard as I jumped up. I placed my hands behind my back and walked out in line behind my team. From the corner of my eye, I could see Hailey giving us a standing ovation, and parents smiling and applauding. I looked for Vanessa, but I couldn't see where she was with the lights shining on me.

When we got offstage and into the back room, we all exploded.

"We did it!"

"YESSS!"

We were all jumping around, throwing our arms around each other. "That was so good!"

"DanceStarz Squad!" Lily cheered.

We went into our ritual, ending by blowing a kiss to one another.

"I messed up a step." Megan frowned.

"I bobbled on my turns," I said at the same time.

No matter how well I did, I always found myself critiquing what I could have done better afterward. Looked like Megan was the same way.

"But you guys killed it on your partner section!" Lily said.

Megan and I lit up.

"I know. I was like this!" I lifted my leg.

"And I slid so close to your leg perfectly—one more inch and I'd have knocked you over!" Megan said. "And then I hinged just in time—"

"So when I kicked over you—"

"I popped up at exactly the right time!" Megan said.

We grinned at each other.

"And Riley, I can't believe you danced so amazingly with an injured hand!" I said.

Riley smiled too.

"And Lily rocked her handstands! And we couldn't have done any of this without Trina and her choreo!"

"Aw!" Trina said. "And you guys executed my new choreo perfectly! We were really in sync."

We all just stood there. I savored the moment, sinking in that we had just performed. My cheeks hurt from smiling so much.

This was what it was all about. It didn't even matter if we won or what place we came in. This feeling was everything, and we didn't even need to know.

*J*UST KIDDING!

I totally wanted to know!

After you dance at some competitions, there might be a lot of time, and you can go chill in the dressing room or sit in the audience and watch the other dances. But today, we were one of the last teams to perform, so we waited offstage.

The judges would be tallying their score sheets. A table would be set up onstage with all of the trophies.

But it wasn't long before a voice came over the loudspeaker through the building:

"Dancers, you are now welcome to join us onstage for awards."

We all went onstage. Lily started to go to the front of the

stage, but Megan and I looked at each other knowingly, and I held her arm to wait. Rookie mistake. Everyone wants to be in the front, especially the little kids and the bigger studios, who would end up all crowded together. We waited until it calmed down, and then found a spot where we could all still see what was going on, but had room for us to stretch our legs out. I had a spot between Lily and Riley, with Megan and Trina next to us.

We had just settled down when a large group filed in and started to plop down right in front of us.

"You've got to be kidding me," Megan muttered.

Yes, Energii. The Bells not-so-coincidentally sat right in front of Megan and Riley.

"Hey!" I protested as Bella sat down practically on my legs.

"Oh, sooorry," Bella said fakely. "Just making sure I didn't crush Riley's hand—like her own teammate did."

Megan froze.

"Ignore her," I whispered in her ear. But I stretched my leg out a little farther, giving Bella a tiny kick. *Oopsie!*

Fortunately, music came on to get everyone pumped up for the awards. We all started floor-dancing along to the music. I waved my arms in the air, then caught a glimpse of my sister, Hailey, in the audience, standing up and dancing around. I waved to her and she waved back.

"I'm so nervous," Lily said.

"It's intense," I agreed. "But so exciting that these are your first awards ever!"

The awards started!

Awards are announced by category. First, the little kids went, so we all applauded for them. Then it was time for our category!

"Put your hands together for our junior groups," the announcer said.

Different dance competitions have different awards they give out. But in most of them, they first announce each dance style and the winners in that category. Then after each category has been announced, the top scorers in each genre compete for the top three.

The first junior category was hip-hop. We cheered as teams were given bronze, silver, gold, or platinum awards. The next was musical theater. We cheered for them, too.

Then they announced lyrical. In front of us, the Energii dancers all grabbed hands and squealed when their name was called:

". . . Energii! DOUBLE PLATINUM!"

That was the highest you could get. It was really impressive. We all were applauding as one of their teammates went to collect a really big trophy.

I looked over to see how Megan and Riley were reacting. They kept their facial expressions neutral. Isabelle and Bella were happily squealing and hugging their teammates. I didn't blame them for celebrating. They did really well. Their team passed the trophy down the row. When it got to Isabelle, she grabbed the trophy and pumped it a few times.

"Double platinum!" Isabelle cheered loudly, holding the trophy right out under Megan's nose.

"Congratulations," Megan said. "That *is* good."

"Good? It's amazing! It's the best!" Bella scoffed.

"I'm SO glad we switched to Energii." Isabelle waved the trophy at us again.

"So am I," Megan muttered.

"What did you say?" Isabelle said.

"Nothing," Megan said. Then she changed her mind. "No, actually, I said, 'So am I.' I'm glad you switched too."

Bella gasped and Isabelle's eyes narrowed. Isabelle opened her mouth to say something, but the announcer spoke loudly.

"May I have your attention now for the next category?"

The dancer sitting next to Isabelle elbowed her to turn back around, so Isabelle had to leave it at that while the announcer continued.

"Our next junior category is contemporary!"

Contemporary! That was us.

"Oh my gosh," Trina said, and she reached over to grab Riley's hand. We all grabbed one another's hands and waited.

"I'm flipping out," Lily whispered to me. I clutched her hand tightly.

I knew it was only our first time. But we'd put a lot into this dance, and we wanted to represent our new dance team! I knew our families were out there, the younger kids from our studio—and, of course, Vanessa.

"And DanceStarz is awarded a . . ." The announcer drew out the suspense. "Platinum!"

Platinum! We all looked at each other in shock. Platinum! That was awesome!

"Whooo!" We all started cheering. Lily and I started hugging each other. Then the Bunheads basically jumped on us and hugged us too.

Megan jumped up and went to accept the award.

"Hi, I'm Megan! I'm from DanceStarz!" she said, grabbing the announcer's mic.

Everyone cheered for her. *Yay!* We were all excited.

Megan came back over and sat down with the trophy. She passed it down to us as they announced the last category, which was tap.

The trophy was red with a silver dancer on the top, and a silvery plate was engraved with the competition name and, in swirly letters, PLATINUM AWARD.

"And now, the moment all of our juniors have been waiting for," the announcer said. "The overalls!"

The overall awards were for the three top scorers, regardless of category. You didn't find out your numbered score until later, so the suspense was killing me!

"We're in it for sure!" Isabelle turned her head toward us and fake-whispered to Bella.

We all ignored her.

With a double platinum, they probably were going to make the overalls. Well, that was the way dance competitions were. You didn't always get what you wanted. We would have to continue to listen to their bragging while we sat there onstage.

"Our top three overall scorers in the junior division! In third place . . . ," the announcer said. Everyone beat their fists on the floor for a drumroll.

"DANCESTARZ!"

I froze. We all froze.

"Am I dreaming?" Lily asked me. "Did he just say us?"

The announcer laughed.

"DanceStarz! Please come up to the front of the stage to accept your award."

IT WAS US!

We all jumped up, cheering.

"Third place?" Isabelle sighed as if that were bad.

"Top three is amazing!" I shot back.

"Not compared to first place," Isabelle said. "Which is what we're going to get."

Whatever.

I was thrilled! This time our whole team got to go up and accept the award. The announcer held out his microphone and asked us, "Tell us, what studio are you from?"

I looked out in the audience and saw Vanessa with a big smile, clapping wildly. I grinned.

"DANCESTARZ!" we yelled into the mic.

Third place stands to the left of the stage, so we went and took our spot. We all had our arms around one another. It was incredible.

"And now, in second place . . . ," the announcer said, "Energii!"

We started clapping for them, but they looked confused. Then several of them frowned. Apparently, they hadn't been expecting second. They all stood up and went to the center.

"What dance studio are you from?" the announcer asked.

"Energii!" they answered. Some were excited, but some seemed disappointed as they took their place at the opposite end of the stage.

When the announcer announced the first-place winners, we all applauded for them. An excited group of girls in dark green outfits who had done a jazz dance went to accept their huge trophy. We cheered them all on. They took their winning spot in the center of the stage, and everyone cheered again.

"Thank you for joining us for awards," the announcer said. "Top three, stay with us for pictures. Everyone else, we will be back in an hour for senior solos!"

It was pretty fun to be able to stay onstage. We lined up as the photographer took pictures of us in front of the competition's backdrop with its big logo over our heads.

"Check out our competition social media to see yourselves!" the photographer said. We were all excited.

After the pictures, our families rushed up on the stage.

"Congratulations!" My mom was the first to reach me. She hugged me hard.

"Thanks!" I said. "I was so nervous!"

My mom's eyes glanced down for a second, and I realized what she was looking at. Oops.

I was twirling my hair. I dropped my hand.

"I know, I'm twirling my hair," I said.

"Harper." My mom smiled at me. "Right now, the only twirling I'm thinking about is your twirling onstage! You were wonderful."

"Thanks, Mom." I smiled.

"You were excellent!" my dad said, and hugged me so hard he lifted me up. "Such talent and grace. Definitely takes after me."

My dad did a silly dance move.

"Dad, you need dance lessons," Hailey scolded him as she came up to us.

"Hmph," he said. "Maybe I'll join DanceStarz."

"Ack, no!" Hailey and I both laughed.

"Let's take a picture to send to your brother," Mom said. "He'll be very proud of you!"

She awkwardly held the phone up to get a selfie with us in it. As usual, it took her a few tries to get everyone in it, not blurry and no blinking.

"Congratulations!" Hailey told me.

"Thanks, Hailey!" I said. I reached out and gave her the kind of hug she liked: an air hug.

"Look!" Hailey showed me her phone. On it was a picture

of Mo, wearing a dog tutu. The caption read: *Woof Woof, Harper!*

"That means 'congratulations'!" Hailey said.

"Wow, that was so nice of Mo." I smiled. It was nice of Hailey to plan that.

"Awww, puppy!" Riley came over and cooed at the phone. Then she looked at my sister and held up her ribbon-bandaged hand. "Hailey, thanks again for my hand wrap! It stayed on perfectly!"

Hailey beamed. That was nice of Riley. Everyone was being so nice!

"How about a group picture with the moms?" my mom said. She made a duck face and threw up a peace sign.

Awkward.

"Yes, let's!" Megan's mom gathered everyone over.

"Mom, I love you," I whispered to her. "But please don't ever make that duck face again."

"Fine," she agreed, laughing.

We all stood with our moms and posed, while Hailey and Quinn held up cell phones.

"Say 'DanceStarz Squad'!" they said.

"DANCESTARZ SQUAD!" we all yelled, and everyone smiled. Megan, too.

"I have a text from Vanessa," Megan's mother said. "She's waiting for you girls in the backstage room."

We all left the stage and walked down the hall toward the dressing room.

"Dance competitions are fun!" Lily said. "Let's do that again."

We all laughed.

"I hope Vanessa is happy with us!" Riley said.

"She should be," I said. "Top three is great."

"Meh," a voice behind us said. Isabelle and Bella had turned the corner and were behind us. "It's okay. It's not as good as top two."

Megan didn't miss a beat.

"Not as good as number ONE, either," Megan said. "Which you probably thought you were getting."

"It wasn't fair." Bella immediately jumped on that one. "We got *double platinum*. There's no way that team's scores were higher than ours."

"We should have won," Isabelle grumbled as we got to the door of the dressing room. "Everyone knows it and—oh, hiiiii!"

She stopped complaining as two older girls wearing lavender leotards came down the hall.

"Senior Energii," Trina whispered to me.

"Congratulations, juniors!" One of them stopped to hug Isabelle and Bella. "Second place! Good effort!"

The other girl turned to me and unexpectedly gave me a hug.

"Um, hi?" I flinched, not expecting that greeting.

"Oh my gosh, sorry!" She squinted at me, stepping back. "I thought I knew you! You looked familiar!"

"No," I said. "I just moved here."

"Wait!" her teammate said. "Aren't you the girl who fell off the float?"

Oh. No . . .

Megan groaned.

There was no getting around this.

"Yes." I sighed. "It was me."

"That is so embarrassing—everyone recognizes you?" Bella laughed.

"I got so many views for that video," Isabelle said proudly.

"You posted that?" the girl asked Isabelle.

"Yeah! She fell off the float right in front of us!" Isabelle cracked up.

"Sooo funny!" Bella laughed. She started to imitate me falling off the float. Her mouth was wide-open and her arms were flailing.

"Soooo mean," the senior girl said.

Bella stopped flailing.

"SO mean," her teammate agreed, frowning. "Also probably against the rules."

Isabelle and Bella looked at each other.

"The rules of Energii," the girl explained. "Good sportsmanship is very important at our studio."

"Uh—"

"I hope you don't get in trouble. Wow, what if you were kicked off the team?" the girl mused.

"I! Uh! Er!" Isabelle was fully in a panic now.

I sneaked a look at the Bunheads. Megan and Riley definitely looked like they were enjoying the show. But Trina looked upset, and I realized what we should do. They needed to work this out for themselves.

"Come on," I whispered to my team. We left them and went farther down the hall, turning a corner toward the dressing room.

"Whew," Riley exhaled. "That was intense."

"That was *great!*" Lily said. "The Bells were shut down. I bet Isabelle is taking the video down right this second."

"That would be great." I smiled. *That would be* really *great.*

Just as we got to the dressing room door, it opened.

Vanessa!

She looked at us. Her face was unreadable. Lily and I had an eye conversation. Was Vanessa unhappy with our performance? Happy?

Vanessa came out into the hallway and looked at us.

"That was beautiful, and I'm so proud of all of you," she said.

Yay!

YAY!

Vanessa opened her arms and hugged all of us. Then the door opened and one of her assistants wheeled out a cart. A little sign on it read: SUGAR PLUMS.

"Fro-yo!" We all applauded.

"Yay, Lily's parents!" Trina cheered.

It was like having a mini–Sugar Plums in the hallway, with frozen yogurt flavors and toppings in cups. I took a vanilla-chocolate swirl yogurt and topped it with cookie crumbles and sour kids. It tasted extra delicious. Once we all had our treats (including Vanessa) and had sat down, Vanessa spoke again.

"Top three is a great way to start," she said. "We'll talk about ways to improve during our next class. But for now, we can be more than satisfied."

We were all smiling.

"However, there's no time to rest. We have our next competition dates! We're going to have a group dance. And we're going to be adding a solo to our competition."

A solo!

We all looked at each other as it hit us. We'd be competing against each other for the coveted solo.

"Who's getting the solo?" Megan was the one to ask.

"That remains to be seen," Vanessa said. "We'll see how the next few weeks go. This will be a great way to prove yourselves."

"Can you imagine?" Trina said. "Having the first solo *ever* for DanceStarz Squad?"

Could I imagine it?

The announcer would say:

"Please welcome to the stage: Harper! Performing . . . A SOLO!"

I would walk onto the stage, my head held high. I would get into my opening pose as the music began . . . five . . . six . . . seven . . . eight!

And I would dance! I would dance, and I would nail it, and I would WIN! And—

I opened my eyes and looked straight at Vanessa.

Yes.

I could imagine it.

$\mathcal{T}$his book is about TEAMWORK, so first I want to thank the team who helped bring this book to life:

• The WME team: Sharon Jackson, Mel Berger, Jenni Levine, Erin O'Brien, Joe Izzi, Matilda Forbes Watson, and everyone at WME for your support and encouragement.

• The Aladdin team: Starting with Alyson Heller, the driving force behind this book—thank you so much! And to Mara Anastas, Mary Marotta, Laura Lyn DiSiena, Carolyn Swerdloff, Jodie Hockensmith, Nicole Russo, and everyone at Simon & Schuster Children's/Aladdin for your hard work and dedication.

• Rachel Rothman, who has believed in me from the very beginning and was invaluable in making this book so awesome!

• Katie Greenthal, Marisa Martins, Elise Mesa, and everyone at 42 West for being such awesome publicists and helping bring my voice out to the world.

• Scott Whitehead and everyone at McKuin, Frankel, Whitehead for all your wise legal advice.

And:

• Julia DeVillers!! You gave Harper (and the rest of the DanceStarz) an amazing voice, and it has been so fun to see these characters come to life. A million thank-yous for being such a smart, savvy, and fun partner on this project!

This book is about DANCE, so of course I want to thank all my friends who have supported me every dance step of the way:

• Sia, who shows me how to be the person I want to be

• All my dance teachers, who have taught me to be the best I can be

• All the dancers who have ever shared the dance floor and stage with me. You've motivated and inspired me!

This book is about FAMILY, and you know I love my family so much!

• Kenzie!! My creative and talented sister. You're my best friend and I love you!!

• Gregga, who has always been there for me, supported me, and made sure I have whatever I need with patience and positivity—and no complaints!

• Jane, Lilia, and Jack Buckingham, who make LA feel like my home.

• Michelle Young, for all the sleepovers, the loud music in the car, and the laughter that never ends.

And:

Mom!! Don't know how I got so lucky to have you as my mom. Thank you for everything.

This book is about FOLLOWING YOUR DREAMS. To anyone who has ever watched me, come out to meet me, bought my books, and cheered me on as I pursue my passions and follow my dreams in dance, acting, fashion design, makeup, the arts—and just living my life . . .

I want you to know I'm cheering you on too. I love what I do so much, so thank you for sharing the journey with me. I love you!

Maddie

About the Authors

Madison Nicole Ziegler, born in Pittsburgh, is an award-winning professional dancer, actress, and fashion designer, and the *New York Times* bestselling author of *The Maddie Diaries*. She starred in Lifetime's *Dance Moms* for six seasons and has starred in numerous music videos for pop singer/songwriter Sia, including the critically acclaimed "Chandelier" video. In 2016, Maddie launched her clothing line, "Maddie." Maddie was also a judge on *So You Think You Can Dance: The Next Generation*, lent her voice to the Weinstein Company's animated feature *Leap!* (released internationally as *Ballerina*), and stars in Focus Features' *The Book of Henry*.

Julia DeVillers is a bestselling author of fiction and nonfiction for kids and teens, including the Trading Faces series with her twin sister, Jennifer Roy, and the Liberty Porter, First Daughter series. Her book *How My Private Personal Journal Became a Bestseller* became the Disney Channel movie *Read It and Weep*.